# BAD BOYS
# EROTIC
# MOTORCYCLE
# CLUB
# ROMANCE

## EROTIC ROMANCE

JENIKA SNOW

SAM CRESCENT

BAD BOYS EROTIC MOTORCYCLE CLUB ROMANCE
Published worldwide by All Romance eBooks, LLC
Safety Harbor, FL 34695
AllRomanceeBooks.com

PUBLISHER'S NOTE
This is a work of fiction and any resemblance to persons, living or dead, or business establishments, events, or locales is coincidental.

ISBN: 978-1-936387-93-9

First Printing, April 2015

# Ridin' Her Rough

## BAD BOYS EROTIC ROMANCE

## Jenika Snow

# CHAPTER ONE

Delilah could already tell there was a party going on inside the clubhouse for the Phoenix MC. The music was loud enough to have her ears ringing, and anytime the front doors were pushed open smoke billowed out from the inside. She had no business being here. After the shitty day she'd had dealing with customers, co-workers who were backstabbing bitches, and getting bailed on by her date only hours before he was supposed to pick her up, all she wanted was someone to talk to. But she wasn't surprised Robbie hadn't wanted to see her when he realized she was the daughter of Carson "Brack" Stringer, the president of the Phoenix MC. The only thing she wanted to do right now was talk about her "girl problems" with Dixon—the woman who was like a mother to everyone at the club. Dixon was old enough to be her mom, and in fact that's pretty much how Delilah saw her. Dixon had been around for the last few years and was the most caring and compassionate person in the club. Those things were something that was lacking in a motorcycle club full of gritty bikers. But now here she was, sitting in the clubhouse parking lot and regretting coming here without calling first.

The door opened again and she saw Ace stumble out. The Phoenix VP was gorgeous in that raw and rough kind of way, and a total man-whore, like the rest the guys. He had a Cherry wrapped around his body. The women who hung around the club were called Cherries, for whatever reason, but one thing Delilah knew is that they would do anything a member asked. Anything. They were sluts, and although Delilah couldn't stand any of them, there were a few with tolerable personalities. She wasn't even going to mention the fact some were only eighteen, and given the fact that was how old Delilah was, it had the ick factor growing in full force. She grabbed her phone out of her purse and dialed the clubhouse number. Hopefully Dixon would answer or no one would pick up, but knowing her luck a drunk member would decide he wanted to get up and actually answer a phone.

"Yeah?" With the music so loud, and the background noise earsplitting, Delilah had a hard time making out who was speaking. It didn't sound like any of the regular members, but as she scanned her eyes over the Harleys lined up in front of the clubhouse, everything inside of her stilled. She would know Torque Morrison's bike anywhere. The black, gleaming Harley had the most elaborate phoenix painted on the side. Flames branched out from its open wings, and the fierce look in the bird's eyes was just the tip of how fearsome the club really was.

"Uh, hey, it's Delilah." She swallowed her nerves and closed her eyes. For the past year Torque had been to the club when he passed through their town of Rush Falls. He was a Nomad, a biker affiliated with the Phoenix MC, but he wasn't locked down with any particular chapter. He was big and hard looking, and so very sexy that just thinking about him had her panties soaked.

"Hello?"

"Sorry. Is Dixon there?" The sound of several women giggling was her response.

"What?" Torque sounded drunker than hell, and like he was starting to get annoyed with the fact he couldn't hear her. Well, that made both of them.

"Is Dixon there?" she said louder. The sound of glass breaking came through and she leaned her head back on the seat.

"Tell whoever it is to go the fuck away."

Delilah gritted her teeth when she heard Pinkie's voice. Pinkie was one of the newest Cherries, and a slut to the nth degree. She also thought her shit didn't stink. There was some shuffling and then Pinkie's voice was screeching through the phone.

"Get a fucking life, cocksucker. Some of us are trying to get laid here." A second later the phone went dead.

Delilah pulled it away from her ear and narrowed her eyes at the damn thing. That bitch. Pinkie slept with everyone at the club, and was clearly about to go after Torque as well. It didn't matter that she didn't know Delilah had been the one on the other end, because the bitch would have acted the same way. She was older, probably in her late twenties if she were to guess, but the bitch thought she was above everyone else when it came to being with the members. And she really looked down on Delilah, for reasons unknown. But she had a feeling it was because of Delilah's connection with the club. Well fuck her.

She climbed out of her car and decided she'd hunt down Dixon and maybe the two of them could go into the office and talk. Torque and Pinkie could go fuck themselves, or each other since that's where it was headed. It wouldn't only do Delilah good, but she knew it would be good for Dixon too. Aside from the few Old Ladies who occasionally came by the clubhouse, and the club whores, it was just the two of them, and Dixon kept to herself when it came to the other women. Her heels clicked on the pavement and she looked at the ground so she didn't inadvertently see something she didn't want to because of the people currently fucking against the side of the building. She gripped the door handle and pulled it open. "Free Bird" blasted from inside and she blinked a few times to focus. There were a shitload of bodies scattered around, the majority of them naked and in the process of some pretty nasty shit. She didn't see Dixon manning the bar or in the kitchenette making any food, so she assumed the woman was hiding out with Ringo. Most likely doing something equally as nasty with the old ass biker.

She moved farther inside and let the door close behind her. She spotted Vain, Malice, Lance, and Mace, and of course all of them were in the middle of some kind of sexual act with a Cherry. "Dammit." Okay, Dixon was obviously not here, and she was clearly not about to stand here watching as everyone got off.

"Fuck, is that you, Delilah?" The sound of Lance's voice was loud enough over the music that she spotted him right away. He was sitting on the couch with a blonde who clearly wasn't a natural one between his legs. Her head was bobbing away but Lance didn't push her away and instead grinned. "Whatchu doing here, girl?" Lance was a prospect, and a dirty old man if she were being honest.

"She's leaving." Vain's voice was right by her ear and she jumped.

She turned and craned her neck back to look at her father's Sergeant of Arms.

"You were just leaving, Delilah. You know damn well this ain't the place for you, and your fucking dad will have all of our balls if he found out his little girl was here." Vain gently took her upper arm.

"Yeah, I was just looking for Dixon, but I'm leaving."

"She should stay. Maybe she could learn something."

Delilah snapped her head in the direction of Pinkie and narrowed her eyes. But her anger toward the woman faded when she saw that Pinkie was sitting naked on top of Torque. Swallowing hard, she couldn't drag her eyes off the sight of him lifting a bottle of Crown to mouth and taking a long swig as he watched her over the rim. He was shirtless, and even with the nude club whore all over him, Delilah could see his tattooed, muscular chest. The dark lines of ink that curved from one shoulder to the next had her eyes riveted to the spot. It was a tattoo all members in the Phoenix MC got, but not the only. She let her eyes run along that menacing dark Old English script that was inked into his skin.

## LIVE HARD. FUCK ROUGH. RIDE FREE.

Pinkie leaned forward and whispered something into Torque's ear, at the same time reaching below to his crotch and rubbing him through his jeans.

"Come on, baby girl." Vain's voice was hard and rough, and she knew she wasn't hiding her emotion well enough.

The flare of Torque's nostrils and the way he stared at her as if he knew exactly what she was going through, and exactly how she felt, was crystal clear. She wanted him, had wanted him for the past year, and it only grew every time he passed through Rush Falls and hung out at the clubhouse. But seeing this club whore all over him was too much, and suddenly she felt pretty damn dirty. Before she could turn and leave Pinkie was sliding down Torque's body, taking out his dick, and started deep-throating him. Vain had his arm around Delilah and was steering her outside before she could see any more.

She shrugged off Vain's hold when they stepped outside and went straight for her car, but stopped, turned around, and stalked back to him. "I should have known this day was going to end shitty seeing that was how it started. And how great there was an audience." Before he said anything she was heading back to her car, starting it, and peeling away from the clubhouse. She was acting stupid. Torque wasn't hers, had showed no interest in her, and was as big a man-whore as the rest of the guys. He was also too old for her, and getting involved with a biker was not something she wanted. The best thing she could do was forget about Torque, forget about what she wanted him to do to her, and focus on getting her degree so she could start a future away from Rush Falls. But she knew that was going to be a hell of a lot easier said than done.

****

*Four years later*

"Fucking hell." Torque slammed his cock back into the female he had picked up at the bar just an hour ago. Her pussy wasn't tight, but she was wet, and easy, so he wasn't going to bitch about some easy snatch. She was moaning like a damn banshee, but Torque had a thing for the noisy ones. He pulled out, looked down at his dick, and saw her fucking cream coating his shit. He thrust back into her hard enough that her whole body fell forward. She had been on her hands and knees, but his forceful actions had her falling into her elbows. With her ass really popped out, he gripped a cheek in his hand and spread that shit wide. Looking down at where his dick was shoved deep inside of her cunt, Torque knew if he wanted to get off any time soon he needed to speed his along. Lifting a hand and bringing it back down on the fleshy mound of her bottom, he spanked the shit out of her. Over and over he brought his hand down, feeling the sting on his palm, but needing more. He needed so much more.

He hadn't bothered turning off any lights in this shitty little room, so he got a prime shot of her reddened cheeks and the nice handprints he left behind. Torque liked the rough kind of sex, the kind that left bruises and scratch marks but always ended in both of them coming harder than fucking hell. Of course, he wasn't about the nonconsensual pain, and the females he bedded with always knew up front what they were getting into if they left with him.

"Harder. Fuck me harder, you bastard." The chick squealed when he did just that, but he gave her a hell of a lot more. She came with a loud cry and he followed right behind, but it wasn't nearly as satisfying as he would have liked.

When she fell forward and was breathing heavily in her exhaustion he got off the bed and went into the bathroom to clean up. Hopefully she'd be gone before he came out. Hell, he didn't even know her name, but she didn't know his either, and sure as fuck hadn't asked. When he had told her leaving with him was only going to end up in an hour of hard fucking, she had been all for it. Just the type of chick he liked to take home with him. Once he was cleaned up he opened the bathroom door and stepped back into the room. Good, she was gone, just the way he liked them to be when he was done with them. Grabbing his jeans off the floor and shoving his legs through them, he grabbed his T-shirt, and then his cut that hung over the back of a chair and put them both on. Being a Nomad for the Phoenix MC meant he had connections, had a place to go if he needed it and brothers to back him up, but he had no roots. That was how Torque liked it.

He didn't want to lay down a home in one specific place. He liked the open road, liked taking his Harley wherever the hell he wanted, even if that meant he spent the night in a fucking field with the open sky as his roof.

Torque had been in the club since he was twenty-one years old, but for the better part of five years he had been doing runs for the Phoenixes located in the Rush Falls chapter. Colorado was a nice state, but definitely not where he wanted to set up shop for himself. With no Old Lady, no kids, and no home, Torque was a forty-five-year-old biker with a nasty ass attitude, a lot of pent-up anger, and the violence that was fueled by that rage. He didn't care who he took out if they crossed his path, didn't care about anything aside from his next stop. Maybe one day he'd slow down, get a nice cabin isolated from others, and live out the rest of his days with his .45 on his right side and a bottle of Jack on his left.

Right now he had to deliver some handguns to the Rush Falls chapter from the River City location, and then he planned on disappearing for a while, just getting lost wherever the road took him. He had about a dozen .38 Specials in his pack that he needed to get to Brack Stringer, the Rush Falls Phoenix MC president. He'd chill for a few days in their clubhouse, hit up a Cherry, one of the free pussy who liked to hang around the clubhouses. They served no real purpose aside from servicing the brothers in any shape, way or form they saw fit, and they sure as fuck didn't expect anything aside from some deep dicking and maybe being picked up by a brother as their Old Lady But that wasn't something Torque would ever delve into. His past and background were far too fucked up to be tethered to a female, and he sure as shit could never give her what she needed: love. But there was only one problem with heading back to Rush Falls, and that was in the form of big tits, long legs, and an ass that was juicy enough all he could think about was fucking it. And that problem happened to be Delilah Stringer, Brack's daughter, and totally off-fucking-limits to Torque, as well as any other member.

Fuck, his dick started to get hard at just the thought of her. She was young as shit, about half his fucking age, and until she hit legal age Brack had done a pretty good fucking job at trying to keep her away from the club. But being the president and having the club be his life meant that was a hell of a lot easier said than done. What really ended up happening was she was at the club more times than not, since that was where Brack was most of the time, the brothers became her family and protected her like she was their own, and Delilah had been the biker brat she had been born to be. When her bitch of a mom dropped her off at Brack's doorstep when she was only three, Brack hadn't known what in the hell to do. But he found out fast enough how to raise a little girl, and now she quickly she became his pride and joy. But Delilah was a hardheaded little thing. Just like her dad. He had seen enough arguments between her and Brack that made him cringe, because if it had been anyone else screaming and pitching fits at the fierce-as-fuck Phoenix president, they'd be six feet under from a bullet wound to their head. But he loved Delilah so much he put up with her shit and finally caved when she had insisted on working at the club and helping out with the books.

Shit, it was pretty fucking sad he knew so much about her, like some kind of damn stalker, but he was close with the Rush Falls chapter, had been since he first joined the Phoenix MC. He had even considered at one point in becoming a full member with them. But he hadn't given that a lot more thought since the idea made him itchy as fuck, and he was afraid he would have done something he would regret, and that would most likely get him killed. He couldn't count the number of times he had passed through Rush Falls, seen her fine-looking ass at the clubhouse, and could only think about fucking the shit out of her. In fact, he thought about the last time he had seen her, which had been four fucking years ago. She had been really fucking young, eighteen and legal, but still pretty fucking young.

Before she had turned eighteen he had noticed the way she looked at him, like she wanted to jump his dick, but fuck, it was bad enough she had been underage and giving him those "fuck me" eyes. But then once she turned eighteen and he had seen her as something more than Brack's little girl, he had known he needed to watch his shit or he'd lose his balls. He remembered that day, even four years later. She had shown up at the clubhouse, and when she had seen what one of the club whores was doing to him the look on her face had done something to him. He had felt like a bastard for the first time in his life. He had watched Delilah grow into a gorgeous woman, but he supposed it had been that one moment when he realized that if he wasn't careful he could really do something that would fuck everything up and piss off a whole lot of people. Delilah had shown a lot of fucking emotion, whether she knew that or not, but he hadn't pushed away the Cherry. The slut had sucked his dick until he had come, and being the bastard he was, Torque had come thinking about Delilah and being balls deep in her cunt. But he had stayed away until right now, let the years pass by, because the things he felt for a girl he should stay away from were suicide. He tried to forget about Delilah and the Rush Falls chapter, but, fuck him, he couldn't. Whatever she had done to him when she looked at him with those big baby blues had changed something inside of him. And Torque didn't fucking like it.

Fuck, he was a sick bastard for the things he had thought about concerning Delilah. It was sick and twisted shit, the kind of stuff someone didn't do to a good girl like her, and would have her screaming and running in the other direction. And Delilah was a good girl, no matter who her dad was or the life she was surrounded by. She was just so damn innocent, and not at all like the loose skanky club whores who hung around and spread their legs at the snap of a finger. What he thought about concerned hard spankings, hair pulling, and feeling her nails rake down his back as he fucked he so hard she was fucking raw from his cock but still begged for more. He palmed his cock through his jeans and cursed. He couldn't remember the last time he beat off. If he wanted to come he just found some pussy, but after thinking about Delilah he didn't even want to taint the image he had of her by finding some loose-as-shit cunt. He unzipped his jeans, pulled out his dick, and braced a hand on the little desk pushed up against the wall. Then Torque did something he hadn't done in a long fucking time. He jerked himself off like some kind of virginal teenager to an image of a female he could never have.

# CHAPTER TWO

Being the daughter of a motorcycle club's president wasn't all flowers and tiaras. There was a lot of shit Delilah Stringer had seen growing up being a biker brat, and a lot of shit she wished she could erase from her memory. But on the tail end of the random sex that went on in the clubhouse, the coarse language, and the violence that surrounded the Phoenix MC on more days than she cared to admit, Delilah wouldn't change any of it.

She parked her Mustang in an empty spot in front of the clubhouse and cut the engine. There was a row of Harleys lined up off to the side, and the huge garage door was open. The garage wasn't a business, just where the guys could work on their bikes and cars. Most of them had a lot of different trades under their belts, the majority being talented in the illegal variety, but they all knew how to fix shit. She stared at Ringo, who got his name because he was a dead ringer for the Beatles drummer. He was currently under the hood of Malice's truck. Climbing out of her car she grabbed the file that held receipts from the "family business" that needed tallied up. The club did a lot of stuff that would land them in prison, and in fact had at some point in their lives.

"Hey." The sound of a tool clanging on the cement was followed by the noise of Ringo hitting his head on something under the car. Delilah shouldn't have laughed, but when Ringo got out from under the truck with grease smeared across his face, she couldn't help it. He was too old to be under any vehicle, but the old bastard liked to keep busy.

"Hey, sweetheart." Ringo greeted her. He was the oldest member in the club, and at seventy-three he looked good for his age.

"My dad here? I didn't see his truck or bike."

Ringo wiped his hands on a greasy rag that would serve little purpose in getting them clean. "Yeah, he's in there. Just got back with Malice." She didn't miss how Ringo didn't give her any more information. It was obviously club business, therefore no concern of hers, even if she was the prez's daughter.

"Okay, thanks." She turned to head inside but Ringo's voice stopped her.

"Just a heads up—"

She looked over her shoulder.

"Pinkie is in there."

Delilah gritted her teeth and forced herself not to groan aloud. Pinkie and her damn slutty ass.

Ringo held up his hands. "Don't shoot the messenger, sweetie. I just wanted you to know so seeing her skinny ass wasn't a shock. I know you two don't get along, and I don't want to know why." No, it never was a shock, because Pinkie had to be the biggest Cherry of them all. She was now in her thirties, but looked rode hard and put away soaking wet. Yeah, her and Pinkie had a nasty little history, one that Delilah wouldn't forget, because that bitch had gotten pleasure in rubbing the fact she had been with Torque in her face. Even all these years later she still made off-the-wall comments about Torque and his big dick, and how she missed him coming to Rush Falls and fucking her ass. That was a problem with these biker assholes. Pussy was pretty high on their list of priorities, especially ones they *thought* were good fucks. Yeah, just thinking about her pissed Delilah off, and ever since then she tended to steer clear of the Cherry or there would be an all-out brawl between them, and Delilah would rip those extensions right out of her bleach-blonde head.

"That bitch needs to get a life and leave the club alone. I don't know why they keep her dirty ass around."

Ringo snorted. "Girl, you know your pop ain't gonna get rid of her unless she really fucks shit up. She's the most popular Cherry in the club, and sucks dick like a damn—"

Delilah cut off Ringo with a firm shake of her head. "No way. I don't want to know any more so don't go there. I already see more ass in this place than I ever needed to in my entire life, but hearing about her—" she shook her head again. "Don't even, Ringo." Most of the guys tried to censor what they said around her because they still saw her as a little girl, but hanging around the club meant there was no hiding anything. Also, Ringo wasn't one to mince his words no matter who a person was. He held up his hands in surrender and turned to finish working on the truck.

Delilah pulled open the door and the scents of beer and cigarette smoke filled the air. It was early in the morning and the lights were dim. The place was a freaking wreck, with beer and liquor bottles, half-naked females sprawled out across the furniture, and yup, there were even some members under those bodies. Dixon pushed a broom across the floor, making a pile of dirt with some condom wrappers and even used ones thrown in there. Delilah wrinkled her nose. She didn't see Pinkie, and most likely she was in one of the back rooms with a member, sucking him off. Ugh, dirty slut.

"Hey, girl." Dixon propped herself up on the broom and smiled. She was an attractive older woman that Delilah was pretty sure was giving lap dances to Ringo. Yeah, that wasn't a sight she wanted to visualize.

"Hey. You're here early."

Dixon rolled her eyes and looked around. There were even a few naked chicks grinding themselves on the members and even the furniture. "Yeah, came in to prep for a big dinner for the guys and their families, but looks like I'll spend most of the morning cleaning up." Dixon shrugged and went back to sweeping. "This is the life I guess."

Delilah shook her head and made her way across the room, stepped over bodies and garbage, and stepped into the office. She shut the door and tossed the file on the scarred desk. The office looked like she had stepped into the seventies with its yellow shag, faded and torn brown chair, and posters on the wall of Farrah Fawcett lookalikes hanging naked over Harleys. Just as she sat in the chair there was a knock on the door.

"Yeah?" Delilah leaned back and looked over at the door.

Dixon pushed it open and leaned against the frame. "You are going to eat dinner here tonight, right?"

Delilah smiled. Dixon was more like a mother to the club, and had been around since before Delilah even came to be part of the Phoenix clan.

"Of course. You know I'd rather hang out with you guys than spend a Saturday night alone at my place."

Dixon gave her a warm smile and the corners of her eyes and mouth wrinkled from the act. At fifty-one Dixon looked old for her age, but her warm personality and caring nature made her seem a lot younger. Delilah didn't know how she had gotten involved with the club but assumed it had something to do with Ringo since no one but him touched her.

"Good. Be back here around eight, sweetheart." She shut the door behind her.

Delilah rested her head on the back of the chair. The thing had to be as old as her and smelled like mold and dirt, but it was one of the most comfortable pieces of furniture in the place. She had thought about leaving Rush Falls, going to college in another city, maybe even Denver or Boulder, but at the end of the day she couldn't do it. So, she had finished school here, gotten her dual business and accounting degree, and stayed in the only place she had ever called home. Now she helped do the books for the club's legitimate business selling hunting equipment to the huge hunting community in this town. The money was decent, but didn't bring in nearly as much as their on-the-side jobs, whatever those may be. Delilah didn't ask were the wads of cash came from because, honestly, she wouldn't have gotten an answer anyways. What she did know was that it was probably blood money, coming from guns, drugs or both. She should have felt guilty and wrong for living this life, but this was the only kind of life that had ever opened their arms and accepted her. Not even her mom had wanted her, but then there were eight big, burly and meaner-than-hell bikers who treated her like she was their little girl when she was only that to one of them. She drummed her fingers on the desk and stared at the water-stained ceiling. There were a lot of fucked-up things in this world, and maybe she was in the thick of it, but hell, she wouldn't change it for anything. Maybe one day she would spread her wings and leave the Phoenixes to start her life in a big city. Oh, who was she kidding? This was her life, and no one left Rush Falls or the MC.

**** 

Torque pulled his bike to a stop in front of the metal gate that blocked off the rest of the world from that of the Phoenix MC. The video camera mounted to the top the wall flashed red, and he stared into it. Seconds later the gate slid open and he drove up the short incline. He backed his bike beside the row of Harleys parked along the side of the building and cut the engine. Dismounting and pulling his helmet off, he looked around. There were a few prospects off to the corner smoking, and a few of his brothers were in the garage looking over the inside of a truck. He whistled and three of them looked up. Torque grabbed his pack off the back of his bike and pressed it to his side. The weight was heavy, but then again that was where the guns were hidden.

The three big ass bikers made their way toward him, and he instantly recognized them. Ringo and his old ass self was limping behind the other two. Ace, the VP, and Vain, Brack's Sergeant in Arms, met him halfway. They slapped each other on the back in greeting.

"Fuck, man, it's been a while since I saw you here, Torque." Ace, with his dark brown hair tied at the nape of his neck, baby blue eyes, and smile that had dropped a lot of fucking panties, was the wooer of this charter. Torque had seen the way he sweet-talked the bitches into going back with him. Hell, there were enough Cherry girls hanging around the club that he just needed to snap his fingers and they'd be on their knees sucking his dick. But nope, Ace was all about talking sweet to the females. For such a Pretty Boy, Ace didn't fuck around when it came to getting the job done, backing up the club, and putting any asshole in his place. If Torque had ever been serious about joining a chapter this was the one he'd pick, hands down.

"Yeah, been on the road for a while. But got a delivery for your prez." Torque looked around. "Where is Brack anyway?"

"He and Malice are inside. He's been expecting you," Vain said and chewed on the end of a toothpick. The sick bastard had his shades on and Torque couldn't gauge the guy's mood. The Sergeant of Arms was a nasty, mean-spirited bastard, but he got shit done, didn't put up with anything, and made some of the shit Torque had done to guys look like a walk in candy-coated fields. Torque supposed that was why he was Brack's right.

He gave Ringo a hug and slapped the old man on the back. They all headed inside. The clubhouse used to be an old warehouse until the club bought it. It had been renovated to house all of the club and their families and keep any unwelcome assholes away. It was on private property with a gate around the entire perimeter, and far enough from the center of Rush Falls that the town didn't fuck with them all that much, but then again they had the police department on their payroll. Shit like that was necessary for them if they didn't want random raids or the cops up their ass when things got ugly. As soon as they walked inside the scents of chili, cornbread, smoke and alcohol slammed into him. The clubhouse was popping with activity, with half-naked bitches all around, grinding their shit on brothers, sucking cocks, or fucking against the wall. "Damn, man, looks like you got the night set up." Torque grunted out and grinned. It was more of a show than genuine.

"Yeah, Dixon ain't too happy." Ace leaned back in his said after he spoke. "She planned this family dinner for the guys and their families, but a bunch of the brothers brought some random chicks home, already half wasted, and that plan kind of got fucked up.

Torque looked over at Ace and cocked a brow.

"Come on, Brack's been asking for you." Vain led them through the fuckfest going on, and every brother he passed stopped what they were doing to greet him. Once they were in the meeting room Vain shut the door and the three of them moved toward the table where Brack and Malice were currently going over some blueprints.

"Damn, man, it's good to see you." He and Brack gave each other a hug. Brack was a big motherfucker, nearly as tall as Torque's own six-foot-three-inch frame, and just as muscular. A lot of the guys in the club were big, whether from working out or over eating, but what they all had in common was they backed each other up, no matter what. Brack grinned broadly, and the scar on his right cheek stretched across his tanned skin. He hadn't shaved in a few days, but neither had Torque, and in fact was thinking of just letting it grow out like half the guys here. "Your ride was good?"

"Yeah, man. Long, but you know I like it that way."

Brack slapped him on the back and nodded. "Yeah, I know."

Torque set the pack on the table, untied the leather, and unrolled it. The .38 handguns gleamed under the lights, and each member grabbed one. They were checked, cocked, and set back on the wool. "The River City chapter said you might have some fun with these."

Ace and Malice chuckled. Vain was still

checking out one of the guns, disassembling it and putting it back together. He was thorough for sure.

"Thanks for hauling it, man. You came on the right night. You see all the hot looking pussy out there?" Malice said.

"I did, but heard Dixon ain't too happy about that." Brack said on a grunt.

"Thought she was going to tan my hide when she saw all the cunt out there, but I had no idea she planned on having a family dinner tonight. That shit would have been useful information ahead of time," Ace said and Torque shook his head and laughed. "She'll get over it, though, especially when Ringo here licks her pussy.

"Shit man, she tastes like fuckin' salt water taffy," Ringo said and there was a collective groan from everyone.

"Ringo, man, quit with the candy reference when you're talking about Dixon's pussy." Ace grinned. "I don't care about you screwing her, but shit, man, I see that woman as a mother figure."

"It aint' my problem the pussy you go after is that young shit that ain't even matured yet." Ringo sat his old ass down at the end of the table. "I'm telling you, boys, you go after some of that fine, aged cunt and you won't ever go back." Everyone cleared their throat when Ringo started making references about Dixon's snatch.

"You're insane."

Malice was grinning over at Ringo when he said this. This brotherly banter was what Torque missed not being stationed in one place, but that was it.

"Pussy is like fine wine. It only gets better with

age," Ringo said and grinned wide.

"This is coming from someone who hasn't had any pussy since Dixon came to the club, and that was like seven years ago. Shit, old man, maybe you should hit up pussy that is young and tight," Ace said. He reached into the inside of his cut and grabbed joint, put it between his lips, and lit the end.

Brack nudged Torque in the shoulder and he leaned in close to say, "You think any more about joining us, brother? We could always use another Phoenix who knows how things run in the club."

Torque looked over at the men still giving Ringo a hard time. "You know I'm not any good with roots, Brack." Torque ran a hand over his jaw after he made that statement.

Brack reached over and slapped him on the back and said, "Yeah, I know. Just know that if you ever change your mind the brothers would love having you come in."

Torque nodded, knowing that was true to the nth degree, but he still had an endgame in sight, and that was solitude and isolation when the time came.

# CHAPTER THREE

Dixon had told Delilah to be at the clubhouse at eight, but it was already nearing ten and she was just now pulling up to the gate. Of course there had been an issue with the invoices she had been tallying up. She punched in the code and while she waited for the gate to open she reached in her purse for cell. Shit, the damn thing was off. Once she had it turned on she saw Dixon had tried calling her a few times and had even sent her a text saying the dinner was canceled.

She drove her car up the driveway and pulled it next to the blacked-out van the club sometimes used for runs. Before she even got out of the car she could hear the sound of Led Zeppelin's "Stairway to Heaven" blaring. A few prospects stumbled out of the garage and their loud laughter could be heard over the music. She scanned the bikes, saw the usual number, but then the very last one in line had her heart beat increasing and her mouth going dry. God, she'd known Torque was going to be passing through, but she hadn't known when. It had been a long damn time since she had seen him—four years to be exact—and seeing his bike right outside the club was like being right back at that night when she was eighteen. Delilah looked at the clubhouse again and realized there wouldn't be any quiet family dinner, but instead an all-out kegger. "Shit." She climbed out of the car and held her covered dish of taco dip. What she should do was get back in her car and drive home. Going in there and seeing a Cherry, most likely Pinkie, all over him once again, would only piss Delilah off, and this time she wouldn't walk away, but finally beat that bitch and her fake blonde ass. Throwing a few punches was a long time coming anyway. "Goddammit." She turned to get back in her car, because she knew what was going on in there, and that was not something she wanted to see, but a deep voice stopped her.

"Hey, Delilah, where you going in a hurry?"

She turned when she heard Vain's voice. He leaned against the side of the clubhouse, hidden in the shadows. The only thing she could really make out was his huge form and the cigarette smoke that billowed out in front of him.

"It looks like there is a bit too much action going on in there for me."

He flicked the cigarette butt away and pushed off the wall. Vain emerged and the shadows moved over him like a blanket falling away. All of the members were big, needing that kind of muscle for what they did, but Vain was a different breed all his own. He was almost as intimidating as Torque, but to her he reminded Delilah of a big brother. They all did.

Vain looked behind him at the main clubhouse doors. "Yeah, it's pretty intense in there." Vain turned back around and grinned. His straight white teeth flashed in the darkness. "Dixon was pretty pissed when a bunch of the prospects and some other members brought home some females. They would have cleared out the clubhouse if she said so, but by then she was already pissed."

"She go home?"

Vain started chuckling and shook his head. "Hell no. Ringo took her in the backroom. I think he probably convinced her that if she gave him a lap dance she'd feel better."

"Ew. I love Ringo, but that's not what I want to hear." Vain laughed at her statement.

"I know, baby girl, but it's funny as fuck to see your face when you hear that shit." Vain might be grumpy to everyone else, but he opened up a little to her, and she knew he only let Delilah see this part. "Besides, Torque came in town and they are getting blitzed in there."

She couldn't help but smile at Vain's words. She looked over at the doors, but of course couldn't see anything. He was in there. When she looked at Vain again it was to see that he watched her intently. Nothing got by the members, and right now she had no doubt spoken loud and clear, just like she had four years ago.

Vain got out another cigarette and lit the end. It burned a brilliant red as he inhaled, and then he exhaled slowly. "You better be careful, Delilah." He took another drag.

"What? I don't know what you're talking about," she asked, but knew what he was talking about before he even responded.

"You do realize that you're shit at lying, right, baby girl? And that you let your emotions come through like a damn race car?" Vain inhaled once more from his cigarette. "How long have I known you, Delilah?"

God, if this was awkward as hell. She stared into the handsome face of the man who had been around for longer than she could even remember. Markus "Vain" Tallmadge was, at fifty-one, a year older than her father, but the only place he wore his age was in his demeanor. He was ruggedly handsome, as were all the other members, but she had always felt this darkness that he harbored inside. It was those shadows that made him a very scary man at times.

"A long time, Vain."

He nodded slowly and took another drag from his second cigarette. "Yeah, since the first day you came into Brack's life."

She swallowed hard when he took another step. She wasn't scared of any of the men in the MC, but there were times she felt intimidated because they could read people so easily.

"You can't hide much, especially from me. The few times I've seen you around Torque there has been that look in your eye."

She shifted on her feet and tightened her grip on her covered dish. "I don't have any look in my eye when he's around." Delilah didn't take shit from anyone, and could hold her own, and that was thanks to the environment she had grown up in, but this was something she was about to back down from. No way was she going to talk about what she really wanted from Torque. It was bad enough that she had never had a real boyfriend. Growing up, the guys who dated her tended to be leery of even holding her hand when they were forced to pick her up at the clubhouse so the guys could "introduce" themselves. To say her sex life was lacking was the understatement of the century. Being a virgin at twenty-two wasn't horrible, but hell, when sex was all around her, and it was those guys banging anything with a vagina, it made them look like hypocrites for thinking she shouldn't have sex herself until she was married and as old as they were.

"I'm not talking about any of this with you, Vain." She tried to sound like this conversation wasn't getting to her, but she knew nothing got past Vain.

He stared at her for a moment, as if appraising what she was thinking, and then shrugged. "Delilah, I'm not your old man, not going to try and father you or give you advice. None of us have any right to harp on you and the choices you want to make in your adult life, but we will continue to protect you." He took another long inhale from his cigarette. "All I'm saying is be careful. Be *very* careful, because you haven't seen the way Torque looks at you when he thinks no one is watching."

Her heart started to race at Vain's words. Torque looked at her a certain way? A way that made Vain point it out to her like a warning.

"And I also want you to remember how you felt when you saw that pussy all over him all those years ago. It hurt you, baby girl, he hurt you, and he will again. It's in his nature. A Nomad don't want anything good and right to settle down with. They want easy and fast, and then they can move on to the next thing. You feel me?"

"Yeah, I understand you, but I'm an adult, Vain. And I know what I should and shouldn't do."

He nodded slowly, and it annoyed her that he wasn't saying anything.

"Nothing is going to happen, ever," she said with a stronger voice and straightened.

He flicked the butt away but didn't say anything for several long seconds. "Good, baby girl, because you know what happens to a member that touches the prez's daughter." He didn't phrase it like a question.

Yeah, she knew what happened, or at least the tip of the iceberg. A beat-down was a given, most likely from her father, but she didn't rule out the other members joining in. She didn't think they would strip him of his patch, but her being Brack's daughter made her forbidden, especially to members of the MC. Delilah had never wanted to be with a member, had never wanted her life to be that deep. And that was what would happen if she were an Old Lady.

"Now, why don't you just head back home and I'll tell Brack you came by?"

She nodded, because that would have been the smart thing to do. Is that what she did? Hell no. "I'm fine, Vain, and in fact will just set the dip down inside for the guys and their beer munchies, grab some files that I can do at home, and then get the hell out of here." She didn't wait for Vain to respond, just walked past him. Instead of going to the front doors she had the brains to go in through the back, away from the party and hopefully not seeing a lot of ass, dick, and tits. The back door was locked, but she grabbed her keys from her purse and pushed the door open when she unlocked it. The back hallway was dimly lit. She didn't bother turning the lights on. She passed closed bedroom doors where the members could crash if they needed. Judging by the sounds of skin being slapped followed by female moans, that wasn't what they were currently being used for. She took a left and headed into her the office, and the sound of the party going on just right on the other side wasn't muted in the slightest. Setting the dish on the desk she grabbed a few files she had forgotten to take with her earlier, shoved them in her purse, and picked up the dish again. She'd just walk into the main area, set the dish on the bar, and head out, all the while keeping her head lowered and her eyes trained on her feet. Heading toward the door she turned off the light and was about to leave when her phone started vibrating. Digging in her purse for it, she stepped out in the hall at the same time she stared at the text that just came through. Before she could read it she slammed into a hard chest, causing her to stumble back and drop the dish. It fell to the ground and the sound of ceramic breaking was barely a blip over all the rest of the noise.

"Oh, fuck, sorry."

Delilah stilled at that deep, baritone voice that instantly had a shiver working over her entire body. She lifted her eyes from the massacre of taco dip on the ground, traveled them up the thighs that were as thick and muscular as tree trunks, and over a flat abdomen that she could see the ridges of his six-pack. She should have been a little stealthier in her appraisal, but it was like her common sense had left her at the moment she heard Torque speak. She lifted her eyes over his broad, flat and equally hard chest, saw the edges of his tattoos peaking over the collar of his white tee, and swallowed the lump lodged in her throat. When she finally made her ascent to his face it felt like she had been staring at him for a long ass time, but she knew it had only been a few seconds.

"I didn't mean to spill your shit, Delilah."

Her pulse raced when Torque said her name. His dark eyes were bloodshot, and the scent of alcohol that came from him was thick. She didn't miss how he swayed to the side, but reached out and placed his palm on the wall right beside her. He leaned in, but it wasn't because he wanted closer to her, but because he had shitty balance right now. But even knowing that didn't have Delilah's arousal lessening.

"It's fine." She swallowed again, but goddammit, the lump in her throat wouldn't budge. His dark hair was shorter than the last time she had seen him, and only reached the nape of his neck. He wasn't handsome in any sense of the word, but more so had this rugged worn look that made his irresistible to her. His nose was straight and his lips were full, his jaw was square, and the dark stubble that covered his cheeks had her thinking about what it would feel like scraping along her inner thighs as he ate her out. *Shit.* She was so unbelievably wet. He breathed out heavily, and lowered his eyes to her lips.

"It's kind of late for you to be out, isn't it?" There was a slight slur in his voice. She knew enough about this type of man that although he was trashed, he still knew what he was doing. He just didn't give a shit.

Delilah glanced around his arm at the archway that led into the main area where the party was going full force, where her father was.

"Baby, no one is lucid enough in there to come save you." He grinned, all straight white teeth that reminded her of some kind of predator. She tried not to let the fact he called her baby affect her, but hell, hearing his deep, slightly scratchy voice saying that one word was like an auditory orgasm. He shifted, and the chain he wore attached to his wallet clanked together. The smell of leather from his cut intensified when he moved.

"I'm not looking for anyone to save me." Even she heard how breathy her voice sounded. The longer she stood there, the more she became a puddle of liquid and jumping to conclusions was a very real threat. She ducked out of the cage of muscle and leather that had just surrounded her, and got on her haunches to clean up the mess. But when she felt Torque's warm, humid breath brush over the nape of her neck and felt his body heat slam into her, she couldn't help but close her eyes. This man was potent, far stronger than any bottle of whiskey or illicit drug. The fact she had lost her mind had her swaying as if she were the one drunk.

She braced her hand on the floor so she didn't fall on her face, but a gasp left her when a jagged piece of broken ceramic sliced right into her palm. Before she knew what was happening Torque had his big hands under her arms and had her off the floor. He pulled her with impressive balance and concentration back down the hallway, and when he found an empty room had her inside of it with the door closed on minutes later.

"Sit." His gruff voice brokered no argument, and when he gently pushed her on the bed so she was forced to sit on the edge of it.

All she could do was stare at him in shock. Blood dripped down her forearm, but before it fell to the floor Torque was back in front of her, kneeling, and had a rag wrapped around her hand.

"I shouldn't have gotten all up on you like that. It was my fault you got all sliced up."

"No, stuff happens." The room was dark, with only the glow from the parking lot lights streaming through the blinds to afford any kind of visual of what was going on. For several slightly awkward moments neither said anything, but she felt his stare on her. Delilah focused her attention on the rag that was wound tightly around her hand. Finally he pulled it off, and she could see the bleeding had already stopped.

He was up and in the bathroom immediately, and then he was back in front of her with a wet cloth and a first-aid kit. "I'm shit at mending others, but have patched myself up plenty of times that I think I could do a decent job." He wiped all the blood away, and the corner of his mouth cocked up.

"Thanks."

He nodded and grunted in response, and now it was her turn to smile. He had her hand cleaned and placed a piece of gauze on the cut that was small as hell for how much it hurt. "You won't need stiches." He wrapped more gauze around her hand, and when it was secure he leaned back.

"I should probably get out there and clean it up." The position he was in had half his face shrouded in shadows, but she saw his gaze trained right on her. "I don't want Dixon to have to clean up my mess." Her words came out far softer than she had meant, but still neither moved.

"I thought maybe you would have been married with a couple of kids by now."

Her cheeks became warm, but she wasn't about to tell him she had neither of those things, and in fact hadn't even gotten past oral while dating. "No. I haven't found anyone that really caught my interest and doesn't piss themselves when they find out who I'm affiliated with. Call me crazy, but I don't want to be saddled with a douche."

Torque chuckled deeply and shook his head.

"But, uh, no Old Lady for you, huh?" She shouldn't have asked that, because honestly she knew he didn't have anyone. She supposed she just wanted to hear him say it. *And for what purpose, Delilah?*

"I'm not really the type of guy to settle down."

Yeah, she pretty much got that. He stood, but because she was still sitting that put his crotch right at level with her face. She curled her uninjured hand into a fist and slowly trailed her eyes up to his face.

"I'm barely controlling myself as it is, Delilah."

Her chest rose and fell with the force of trying to get enough oxygen into her lungs, but she was growing lightheaded regardless. "What?" It seemed when her lust pounded inside of her she was nothing more than a one-worded kind of girl, but this man made her this way, and she knew he always would.

"Baby, if you keep looking at me like you want me to fuck you, then that's what I'm going to do." He curled his hands into tight fists and she watched as his jaw hardened. "In fact, I've had enough to drink that even though I know what I want to do to you will likely get my ass handed to me by your dad and the other members, at this point I am so fucking hard-up for your pussy I don't even care."

Her tongue felt swollen, as did the rest of her damn body. Her clit throbbed, and her nipples were so damn hard she wouldn't have been surprised if the damn things ripped through the thin material of her top. "I think you're too drunk to know what you're saying." She needed to get out of this room right now or she'd be liable to do something that would most likely end up having her regret this in the morning. They were now face-to-face, and although they were only inches apart, Torque didn't move. He was at least a foot taller than her measly five-foot-two-inch frame, and so she was forced to crane her neck back to look him in the eye. God, he was just so big and masculine, and although Delilah wasn't a little thing by any means, even considered herself more on the thick side, this man made her feel petite in every way imaginable. Before she could move away he shot his hand out, grabbed a chunk of her hair, and yanked her head back until her throat was bared to him. The sting of pain from his forceful touch only amplified the lust burning inside of her. She parted her lips, not knowing if she was going to tell him to stop or beg him for more.

"Baby, I know what the fuck I'm saying, and who I'm saying it to." He leaned in close until she felt the brush of his lips along hers. He didn't add any pressure, just held them there like he was some kind of sadist and was getting off on the fact that she was squirming from his torture. "I know that if I were to fuck the prez's daughter, I'd get a fucking beating that would probably leave me bleeding out of my ears." His breath was warm and smelled of whiskey, but the sweet scent had her pussy clenching. "But you know what, baby?" He didn't give her a chance to speak. "I have wanted your ass for far longer than I am even comfortable admitting, and I know you want my dick buried deep inside of that sweet little pussy of yours too."

"Oh, God."

He chuckled deeply and shook his head, which had his lips brushing back and forth along hers. "No, Delilah, not God. But I'm going to have you calling out his name as I fuck the shit out of you." He crushed his mouth against hers in an almost brutal way, and pressed his hard, big body into hers. He tightened his hands in her hair, tugging at the strands until the pain morphed into pleasure and all she could think about was giving herself to Torque any way he wanted. It didn't matter that she had never had sex before, that she would most definitely be losing her virginity to this hardened biker that knew far too much about sex for her comfort, but that had the expertise to make sure nothing was left out.

He used his massive body to push her back on the bed, but even with the momentum of them hitting the mattress, Torque never broke the almost violently aroused kiss he was giving her. He moved his tongue in and out of her mouth, fucked her between the lips like she desperately wanted him to do between her thighs. He tasted like alcohol and smelled like motor oil. Delilah didn't particularly like that smell and flavor, but shit, it turned her on so much she was a wet, aching mess between her thighs. His erection was huge as it pressed against his jeans and right into the hot, throbbing spot between her thighs. God, if he felt this big through pants she could only image what he would feel like pushing all of that inside of her. His hands were everywhere, moving over her arms in an almost bruising manner, and over her chest until he had her breasts in his hands. He broke the kiss and leaned back enough to look at where he groped her.

"Fuck, your tits are so fucking big. I was always a man who thought the saying 'more than a handful is a waste' a load of bullshit." He flicked his gaze to hers and squeezed her breasts hard enough that a flash of pain filled her, but also had her nipples hardening in pleasure. "I'm going to titty fuck these until I come all over you, baby."

Her pulse drummed in her eyes and she wanted him now. He thrust his dick against her pussy, and a silent cry left her when he rubbed up against her clit. The hard bundle grew even more swollen, and she knew that it wouldn't take much to get her off.

Torque moved away so he was on his haunches, and let his eyes move between her legs, over her breasts that strained against her top, and back up to her face. "You want this, baby? You want my dick deep inside of you, pounding the shit so that every time you sit down for the next week you'll know I tore that shit up?" His voice was dark and rich, caressing her body until she was seconds away from begging him to fuck her. "Get naked. Let me see those big ass tits."

There wasn't a part of her that was saying this was a bad idea. She pushed her upper body up, grabbed the edge of her shirt and pulled it up and over her head.

"Now the bra." His eyes were locked on her chest, and she flicked her gaze down to the bulge about ready to burst through his pants.

Reaching behind her for the clasp of her bra, she undid it, and pulled the straps off her shoulders, down her arms, and tossed it aside. The room was dark enough that she didn't feel self-conscious about the fact her belly was thicker than she liked, because the way Torque stared at her made her feel like she would burn alive. "I've—"

He shook his head, stopping her from saying anything more. "No, baby. I don't want to talk. I've wanted you for a long fucking time, and I'm not going to deny myself any longer." He pulled his shirt off, and the yellowish glow from the lights outside had lines of slashing across his chest. God, it wasn't just a chest, not with the hard muscle that flexed and bunched, or the flesh he used as a canvas for all of his ink. His massive arms were covered with different designs from shoulder to wrist. Right in the center of his chest, below the club's saying, was the MC's brand. It was a phoenix rising from the flames, and below that in hard block letters was the club's name.

Delilah had always been used to this type of male, this breed that was more masculine, hard, intense and raw than anything else. She just hoped she could handle what Torque was about to give her, and prayed that when this was all said and done it wouldn't be the worst mistake she had ever made.

# CHAPTER FOUR

Torque couldn't control himself around Delilah. Not when the alcohol pumped through his veins with more intensity every time his heart beat. He knew what he was doing, knew she was Brack's daughter, but he just didn't give a fuck. He should, but he didn't. He had her jeans off in a matter of seconds, and had his hands on her knees, wrenching them open so he could get an unobstructed view of her panty-covered cunt. Her body was made to be fucked hard. She was all curves, all woman, and he was about to do some serious damage to her that would have her clawing at his back and screaming out his name. "Lay on your back." It was taking a lot of self-fucking-control to not rip his fucking pants off and shove his dick deep inside of her. He needed to go slow, because she seemed pretty fucking innocent and nervous, and the only thing that made sense was the only guys she had ever been with had been those pansy ass motherfuckers that she had gone to school with. He kept his hands on her knees, and slowly slid them down her inner thighs, and stopped when he could frame her pussy with his fingers. The material of her panties was soaked right through, and his mouth watered for a taste. Placing a hand on her rounded belly, Torque curled his fingers into her butter-soft flesh and didn't hold in his groan. His dick throbbed, and he could feel the wetness from his pre-come start to seep through his jeans. He couldn't remember a time when he was this hard up for a female.

"Torque."

The way she said his name, all needy and desperate had him moving between her legs, lowering her head, and placing his mouth right on her cunt through the material of her underwear.

"Christ, Delilah. You taste so good." The sweet, musky flavor of her filled his mouth and he groaned against her.

She gasped, no doubt from the vibrations, and he wanted more from her. Torque wanted her screaming as she came, and he'd have her doing that soon enough. He tightened his fingers into the area where her thighs met her pussy, and knew there would be bruises, but this primal, male part of him wanted his mark on her, and that was something he had never experienced before. He found her hard little clit through her underwear, and sucked it into his mouth until she writhed beneath him. He couldn't take it anymore, because he needed to taste her bare flesh. Pulling back and hooking his thumb on the side of the material, he jerked it aside, exposing her completely nude pussy lips. "Fuck, baby." He ran his finger along one slippery, smooth lip, and then did the same with the other. "Damn, I like my pussy hairless, and yours is goddamn perfect." He latched his mouth onto her creamy cunt, and she instantly speared her hands in his hair and tugged at the strands. He grunted against her flesh, but she must have taken that as he didn't like it because she let her hands fall away. "No, Delilah, fucking pull my hair, make it hurt, baby."

Her breathing increased and she put her hands back in his hair, tugging at the strands once again. When he had his mouth back on her clit, and his tongue stroking over the swollen bundle of tissue, she really fucking pulled at his hair. He hissed out, groaned out for her to do it again, and was pleased when she obeyed.

"It's good, Torque. God, it's so good."

Yeah it was, but he had a lot of other things planned for her. In one swift move he tore her panties the rest of the way off and feasted on her cunt. He pulled her labia apart with his thumbs, flattened his tongue and ran it up and down her slit. When he placed the tip of his finger at the opening of her pussy, her entire body tensed. She was tight as shit as he worked that one finger into her, and the rhythmic pull of her inner muscles clenching around the digit had him nearly coming. He added another finger until all he could think about was hid dick replacing those fingers, and her tight-as-sin cunt milking his cock until he came something fierce. He had only gotten to the first knuckle of a finger fucking her before he couldn't take it anymore. Wrenching away from her and going at the button and zipper of his jeans like a fucking man insane, he tore that shit open and worked them off. When he was just as naked as she was and he saw the way she stared at his cock, he couldn't help when the damn thing jerked forward. "Baby, there isn't anything to be nervous about. This right here—" he held his hard cock in his hand, and ran the pad of his thumb over the Prince Albert piercing at the head of his shaft, "—this will only make shit feel a whole lot better."

Her chest rose and fell, causing her breasts to jiggle and sway from the force. He scrubbed a hand over his jaw as he watched the soft, spongy mounds bounce slightly. He was right back between her legs, with his mouth on her clit and his hands on her inner thighs. She'd get off before he fucked her. He'd make damn sure of it. Over and over he licked her, feeling her tremble beneath him the closer she got to coming.

"I'm so close, Torque."

Her words were broken up and harsh, and he lifted just his eyes to her while he kept eating her sweet cunt out. It got to the point that the only way he could relieve some of the tension in his shaft and balls was to dry hump the damn mattress like some kind of teenager. Over and over he pressed his hips into the bed, urging her with his tongue, mouth, and hands to come. "I need this, Delilah. Fuck, I need you to come all over my mouth." He reached up, took hold of her nipples with his thumb and forefingers, and pulled on the tips. He twisted and tugged at the tips until she moaned out long and loud, and finally gave him what he craved. Her orgasm was as sweet as the rest of her, and he swallowed that shit up, loved the fact he was the one who caused her to come this hard. It was only when she started pushing at his shoulders did Torque force himself to stop. He sat up and took in the way she looked pleasurably exhausted, splayed out for him. "Fuck, you're so damn hot."

She opened her eyes and the smile she gave him couldn't be called anything but tempting. He left her only long enough to grab a condom from his wallet and slide it on. He was right back between her legs, moving his hands up and down her legs, knowing he wouldn't fucking last long.

"Get on your fucking belly, Delilah."

"Torque, there is something you need to know."

He snapped his eyes to hers, barely holding on as it was, and she wanted to talk? "You have an old man?"

She shook her head.

"You pregnant?"

Again, she shook her head.

"And you're clean?"

After she nodded he shrugged. "There ain't nothin' to talk about, baby. You want me to fuck you, and I really, really want to fuck you." He gripped her waist and easily flipped her on her belly. As soon as her ass was right in his damn face he brought his open palm down on it. She snapped her head around and looked at him over her shoulder. He stared at her right in the eye, held his hand out, and said, "Ask me for it, Delilah."

She licked her lips, looked over at his hand for several seconds, and then brought her eyes back to him.

With his other hand he went between her legs and ran the digits through her overly slick cleft.

"You want it as badly as I want to give it to you. Now, fucking ask for it, baby." His balls drew up tight to his body.

"Give it to me, Torque." She breathed out.

And that was the only thing he needed to hear. He spanked the right cheek twice before moving to the left. He alternated between the cheeks until even in the darkness he could see the way her ass was a brilliant red from his actions. She lifted her ass, spread her legs wider and begged him for more.

"I want it harder. God, what is wrong with me." She didn't phrase it as a question, and she sure as hell didn't sound ashamed or frightened that she liked a little pain with her pleasure. She was perfect. Absolutely fucking perfect. She rested her head on the bed, turned it to the side, and watched him as he continued to erotically abuse the big, round mounds of her ass.

Torque's mouth watered for a taste of her ass, to see if her tight hole was as sweet as her vice-like pussy. Giving each cheek one more hard slap, he gripped the flesh, pulled it apart, and stared at the dark crease between them.

"W-What are you doing?" Now she sounded hesitant.

"Anyone ever taste you back here, Delilah?" Even he could hear the harsh note in his voice, but there was nothing Torque could do about it. He felt like a damn feral animal hunting for its prey. Delilah was that prey, and she was ripe for the picking. "Has anyone, baby?" He curled his fingers into her skin, eliciting a little pain.

Her eyes widened and she shook her head. "No. No one's touched me."

The way she said that had him stilling. He pushed anything that didn't have to do was taking this hot piece of ass in front of him. But on that thought, and as he looked into her eyes that looked dark in this room and not their usual bright blue, he felt something else. It was a feeling that he had buried deep, knowing that it had no place in his life. It wasn't love, but it was something akin to it, something that scared the shit out of him. Torque pushed it back down, buried it deep inside of him, and only focused on the physical reaction. He had no time for emotional bullshit. "Well, I'm about to show you a few things then, baby." Leaning in slowly, he closed his eyes and inhaled deeply. Yeah, her ass was going to be just as sweet as the rest of her. Torque placed his tongue right on her pussy hole, dipped it inside of her a few times, and then dragged it up her crack and stopped when he got to her anus. The hole was small and puckered. The scent of her soap filled his nose. It was lemony and fresh, and a groan rumbled from him. Licking and sucking, teasing and opening, Torque started out gentle in pleasuring her, and when she finally relaxed back on the bed and started lifting her ass into his face, that was when he really started to lose control. He was a fucking madman on her ass, fucking her with his tongue until she was a squirming mess beneath him, and her pussy cream made a tantalizing wet spot right on the mattress. Rubbing her clit once more and rimming her out, Delilah came seconds later. That was as long as

Torque could last. He moved away from her, wiped his mouth with the back of his arm, and reached out to flip her onto her back. Her tits bounced from the force of his movements. "You ready for this?" It was a rhetorical question, because if Torque didn't get his cock into her his balls were sure to explode.

"God, just fuck me already," she begged.

Hands on her waist, he wrenched her down the bed until her ass hung off the edge of it. Taking hold of the root of his cock, he aligned the tip at the opening of her pussy and looked into her face once more. Even through the condom he could see the big, hard ridge of his piercing, and when he pushed just the head inside of her a grunt of pleasure left him when her small opening started to stretch wide around it. For a moment he just stayed in the position, with half of his cockhead inside of her, because though he wasn't thrusting, it felt really damn good to be inside of Delilah. He had wanted this for a long time, had thought about it, fantasized, and jerked off to the images in his head. But none of those things could compare to actually having her pussy clenching around his erection. He should have gone slow, and he realized that he was starting to say that a lot now that he was finally with her. But just because he thought he should go slow didn't mean he could actually do that. In one quick and euphoric filled thrust, he buried all of his length inside of her. Her eyes grew pretty fucking big, and her mouth opened wide. Shit, maybe he should have gone slow, and worked his shaft into her? But fuck, she was primed for him, and he didn't have the patience to wait. The alcohol was still pumping through his veins but he wasn't drunk enough to not realize that he had just popped her cherry. He stilled inside of her, feeling the scorching hot tightness of her inner walls cutting the fucking blood flow off.

"Motherfucking hell, Delilah." Sweat broke out along his brow. "Why didn't you fucking tell me you were a virgin?" The feel of him breaking through her hymen had been unmistakable, even in his slightly inebriated state. She squeezed his dick especially hard and he hissed out a breath and groaned. "*Christ*. You can't do that shit and expect me to keep my shit together." He opened his eyes and saw the fierce look on her face.

"Are you going to fuck me or have you lost your hard-on because you popped my cherry?"

For several seconds he was stunned speechless. The little tart had a fucking mouth on her. He pulled out, and shoved back into her hard enough that she moved an inch up the bed. A gasp left her and tears filled her eyes and spilled down the corners of her eyes. "Shit, I'm sorry, baby." He reached out and brushed a few strands of hair from her face.

She shook her head and he pulled his hand back. "Don't ruin it by being sorry. I've wanted this for a long damn time. Just fuck me and make it memorable."

Damn. Her words were like a spear right in his gut, and that was the first time a female had gotten through his skin with a few choice words. "Fine." He gritted his teeth as he slowly pulled out, and then equally pushed back in just as slowly. Over and over he did this, and although he really wanted to bang the hell out of her Torque forced himself to go slow.

"Faster. I want it faster, Torque, and harder." Shit, she was a damn nympho, and this was her first time.

"I don't want to hurt you." He didn't stop thrusting into her. Both of them were out of breath, and the sweat on their bodies was making the most delicious sloppy sounds.

"The pain has passed, and I'm going to be sore no matter what. I want to fucking remember this every time I sit down."

Well fuck him. This chick was crazy hot, and all fucking his for the night. Before she started running her mouth again he had her in his arms, turned around, and pressed against the wall. His dick was still in her, but this new position had him able to go deeper, and when he did just that and the soft mewling noise left her he felt his dick harden impossibly further. He fucked her against the wall, had a tight grip on her ass, and knew he'd come if he didn't slow down. But he didn't want to go slow, and he didn't want to come yet. She felt incredible, and this would definitely be one of those times that would have him thinking about her every time he fucked another bitch. But on the heels of that thought was another one. It was one that beat in his skull that he had never thought about a female, wanted the same one, and fantasized about for four fucking years. Yet he had done all of those things concerning Delilah.

"It's good. God, I think I'm going to come again."

"Yeah, baby. Fucking come all over my cock. Milk me until there isn't anything left." He had a hand on each of her ass cheeks, holding her up, but using her bottom as leverage as he bounced her up and down on his dick. The wet, sloppy sounds of her pussy sucking at his erection was an auditory aphrodisiac that had him right there, ready to fucking spew forth the biggest load he had ever had. "Now, Delilah, fucking come now."

She tossed her head back and it banged on the wall, but the sound of her low wail had him coming right along with her. "Torque, oh fuck, Torque."

Yeah, that's it. Calling out his name was music to his ears, and a spike of lust to his dick. When her tightness, and the fact he had come harder than he ever had, started to claim him, he slowed his pace and rested his forehead against the crook of her neck.

She panted against him, and it was just now that he realized she had her hands wrapped around his neck and her lips by his ear. "No regrets."

He didn't know if she was talking to herself or him, but he didn't say anything because honestly he didn't know what to say. He pulled out of her with a hiss and set her gently on the ground. For a moment all they did was stare at each other. Torque lifted his hand and ran his thumb over her forehead, down her temple, and followed the line of her cheek to her jaw.

"I can't even tell you how that was." She smiled up at him and his chest grew tight. Shit, he wanted her, but it wasn't just for this one time.

He really fucking wanted her, wanted to do this again, and hold her afterward, and talk to her about shit that didn't really matter. "I know." He leaned down and kissed her forehead. "I'm going to get cleaned up." Damn he could look at her all fucking night and never get tired of the sight of her. Before he did something dumb like express his feelings, Torque turned and headed to the bathroom. Once the door was shut and the irritating florescent light was on, he braced his hands on the edge of the sink and stared at his reflection. He was getting too fucking old for this shit, and the fact that he was thinking about being with Delilah for more than just one night was insane. Even if Brack didn't kill him for touching his daughter, for fucking taking her damn virginity for Christ's sake, Torque had always told himself he didn't need or want an Old Lady. He was content by himself, riding alone with only his thoughts to keep his stubborn ass company. He was happy living that life. Right?

Letting his head hang between his shoulders he thought for several minutes on what in the hell he was going to do. If he were being honest with himself he knew that walking away from Delilah wouldn't help him forget about her, or the fact he had been trying almost desperately to purge her from his thoughts. Whatever it was about her was not something he could just push off as being hard up for her pussy. In fact, taking her pussy had made him feel this proprietary need for her, and just the thought of any other asshole sticking their dick in what was his had him damn near homicidal. He wanted Delilah, and for more than this one night. It may not have been what he wanted in life, or what he thought he needed, but thinking about riding without her on the back of his bike was uncomfortable in a way he had never felt before. What had started four years ago with one look of pain on her face had slowly grew inside of him, worked its way into his once cold and hardened heart, and came to an explosive ending when he had claimed her. And Torque had claimed the shit out of her. They needed to talk, and Torque needed to find out where Delilah saw this going. Because Torque sure as hell didn't want to walk away, even if the club brothers beat the shit out of him for touching what was off-limits.

# CHAPTER FIVE

Delilah grabbed her shirt and bra off the floor and quickly put them on. Her panties were torn in half and useless, but she picked them up regardless because no way in hell was she leaving these lying around. When she found her pants she was in the process of pulling them up when the bedroom door was pushed open. The light from the hallway had the front half of the person shrouded in darkness, but Delilah didn't need to see the face to know it was Pinkie standing in the doorway.

"Well what do we have here?" A few seconds later the sound of heavy boots coming down the hallway preceded the big form of her father stepping up behind the bitch. "Brack, baby, looks like this room is taken. We'll have to fuck somewhere else."

Pinkie grinned and Delilah narrowed her eyes. That bitch. Her father pushed the Cherry out of the way and flicked on the light. Just standing there her dad was a scary-looking guy, but when he was pissed people better clear out of his path because shit was about to hit the fan. And that anger he kept a tight rein on morphed his face as he looked her up and down. He turned his attention to the bed, which had the appearance of just being fucked in. It was only a second that had passed before he snapped his eyes to the bathroom where running water could be heard. She could see the way his entire body tensed, saw him tighten his hands into fists, and heard as he cracked his knuckles.

"What the fuck is going on here, Delilah?" Her father turned his head to her direction and pierced her with the same blue eyes she saw every day when she looked in the mirror.

"It's, uh…" God, how in the hell was she going to explain this? It was bad enough that her dad had come to this room so he could fuck the club slut, but even worse that he caught her in her after-sex state. Delilah supposed it was better than Brack walking in on her actually doing it. Her heart thundered and she slowly shook her head. She had no clue how to proceed. It was stupid of her to have sex with Torque in general, but really stupid to do it at the clubhouse. She had known better, yet hadn't cared because she had wanted Torque too badly, and she supposed it was her pent-up desire that had spanned four years that had made her throw caution to the wind.

"Delilah, you need to tell me what the hell you're doing in one of these rooms with your hair all fucked up, the bed looking like it was put through the damn washer, and your clothes all jacked up." Her dad's wide, big chest was rushing and falling quickly from his anger. Pinkie stood in the hallway, her arms crossed under her chest, and her big, fake tits nearly spilling out of her elastic top. She also had this shit-eating grin on her face, and it was clear she was enjoying the hell out of this.

Before Delilah could say anything the bathroom door opened. She started at Torque, who was still butt fucking naked and semi-hard, and her eyes widened in fear.

"Baby, we needed to talk about what the hell just happened." His head was downcast, and she could see his brow furrowed as if he was thinking hard. When she didn't respond he lifted his head. Torque stopped instantly, stared at her, and then moved his eyes to Brack. His body got just as tense as her dad's had, and with both of the men equally tall and muscular, Delilah knew that what was about to happen was going to end in a lot of blood being spilled. Shit, this was not good, and things were about to go from really bad to pretty fucking shitty.

****

*Fuck.* That was the only thing that went through his mind when he saw Brack standing just inside the room with a murderous expression on his face. There was no denying that he had just fucked the club president's daughter. Hell, Torque was still naked with his dick half hard. He didn't move, and sure as hell didn't let his guard down. Shit was about to get real, but Torque had known that messing with Delilah would end in this result. Even if Brack hadn't found out, Torque was going to talk to her about taking shit to the next level, to seeing if she wanted to be his Old Lady, and to give whatever it was that had been brewing between them for years a shot. He saw Delilah move closer to him, and a second later his jeans were tossed to him.

"Dad, before you start jumping to any conclusions let me explain."

Torque put his jeans on but never took his eyes off Brack, and the prez kept his icy glare on Torque the whole time too.

"There isn't anything to explain, Delilah. I don't need to be a genius to realize a brother just fucked my little girl in *my* fucking clubhouse." Brack's voice was booming, which drew the attention of Ace, Malice, and Vain, who now stood right behind Brack. The prez took off his cut, and Ace was right there to take it. Brack cracked his knuckles, rolled his head on his neck, and grinned. "I'm going to fuck you up, boy."

"Please. Dad, you don't have to do this. I'm a damn adult and have the choice to have sex with whomever the hell I want." Delilah's voice was raised, which had a few of the brothers lifting their brows in surprise. Torque knew they were more entertained at the fact this little female was standing between two hulking bikers.

"Baby, step back. This needs to happen if anything between us is going to move forward." Even with the pumping music in the background, everything became deathly silent at Torque's words.

"She's not your baby, and there isn't anything going on between the two of you, and sure as fuck won't be moving forward."

Torque had his attention on Delilah even though Brack's words were low and menacing. She didn't speak, but her shock was evident in her eyes.

He picked up his jeans and put them on. He knew shit was about to get gritty. All he could do was smile at her, because this little revelation was a big shock to him as well. "Delilah, move back." He reached out and pushed her aside gently, but that still had a low growl coming from Brack.

"How long have you been fucking my daughter behind my back?" Brack still didn't move, but he was just as juiced up for this fight as Torque was.

"I haven't been doing this behind your back. This is the first time I've been with her, but I won't lie and say it'll be the last. I also won't lie and say I haven't been thinking about being with Delilah since she was eighteen years old."

"Oh shit."

"Man, Torque, why did you have to say that shit?"

The comments came from the other members fast and furious, but they stayed put, knowing this was about him and Brack. But what he said was clearly Brack's breaking point because he charged forward like a damn rhino intent on taking a tank down. But Torque was ready for this shit. Torque met him in the middle of the room, and as soon as they reached each other the fists started flying. Delilah was screaming something at them, but Torque saw Vain pull her away from the carnage that was happening. Brack popped him in the jaw and Torque stumbled back.

"You fucking asshole." Brack swung at him again but he caught the president in the gut. He grunted in pain.

Torque slammed his fist into his jaw. "I'm not

giving her up." They sparred for several minutes, both of them of equal size and strength and neither one of them submitting.

"She isn't yours, Torque." They fell to the floor and the fists were flying faster than either of them could keep up. Brack got him in the right kidney at the same time Torque gave him an uppercut. They both broke away, blood dripping down their faces, lips busted the fuck up, shit bruising and swelling. "She isn't yours, man. You are a Nomad, never staying in one damn place and not caring about shit." Brack pushed himself up, but he didn't come after Torque. He did the same, and the two of them stared at each other.

"She's different. I knew it four years ago, but it didn't register until right now when I thought about leaving her behind."

"What, you mean after you fucked her?" Brack spit out a mouthful of blood.

Torque ran the back of his arm across his lips, saw the blood covering his forearm and sighed in defeat. "I meant no disrespect, brother, really I didn't. I also didn't plan this shit. It just happened." He looked over at Delilah, who had a horrified look on her face.

She shrugged off Vain's hold and stepped closer. "Dad." She waited until Brack turned around and looked at her. "I can only speak for me, but I knew what I was doing, and wanted this." She looked over at Torque for a moment, and then turned her attention back to her dad. "I care about him, have for years, and up until tonight I made damn sure I keep all of that shit to myself. I don't want anyone fighting because he wasn't supposed to do this, or do that. I'm an adult, and I think I deserve to make my own decisions."

"Baby girl." Brack sighed and lowered his head so he was looking at the ground. "This shit ain't good. He's too old for you, and he wants no roots. The only thing a Nomad wants is the open road."

"Age is just a number. Besides, I know my mom was only nineteen when she got pregnant with me. That made you thirty-one. It's all just a number, Dad. You know that. Look at Ringo and Dixon." Brack shook his head from side-to-side, but didn't say anything. "And maybe I'm stepping over some kind of biker, brotherhood line, but don't I have the right to choose who I want to be with? Haven't I earned your respect?"

The room grew tense at her words, and when Brack slowly lifted his head to stare at her, Torque knew that Delilah had reached a part of him that few had touched.

"Yeah, baby girl, you've earned my trust, as well as the club's, and a whole lot more." He reached out, tucked a strand of dark hair behind her ear. Brack looked over at Torque, and even though he still had a hard look on his face, there was something in his eyes that he had never seen in the club president before: surrender. "You care about my daughter?" He turned fully around so they were face-to-face again.

Torque looked over at Delilah, but she had her head downcast, like she didn't want to look at him. "Yeah, prez, I really fucking do." He looked at Brack in time to see the man coming closer.

"She's my baby girl." They were only inches from each other, but Torque wasn't going to back down.

"Yeah, I know, man."

Brack nodded once. "If you hurt her I will hurt you." The threat was very real, but Torque wouldn't have had it any other way.

"I understand, but there is no way I'm going to hurt her. She's the first female I've wanted as an Old Lady, and you should know that isn't something I would ever fuck around with."

Brack grunted and searched Torque's face with his eyes. "Yeah, I guess I know that, but what you're messing with is not some club Cherry."

"I want this with her, Brack." They stared at each other for several long minutes.

Brack nodded once, turned and staked out of the room. The rest of the guys stared at them as stunned as Torque felt, but they didn't say anything. Ace smirked, Malice shook his head, and Vain watched Torque like he was some kind of fucking experiment.

"You watch over her, brother." Vain pointed his finger at Torque, and then turned and left.

He breathed out, not realizing he had been holding his breath.

"Shit." Scrubbing a hand over his jaw, he felt like he might fucking pass out. He had just claimed Delilah in front of the club.

"Torque." Delilah was right in front of him before he even realized what the fuck was happening.

"Yeah, baby?" What if she wasn't all about

what he wanted? What if this really had been just one night of sex? Yeah, he had heard what she said, but shit, didn't chicks change their minds all the fucking time?

"Did you mean what you said about me and you?"

For a moment he just stared at her. Fuck, she was so beautiful. Her dark hair was mussed from what they had just done, her lips were red and swollen, and she stared up at him like she wanted to do this all over again. "Yeah, Delilah, I meant every word of it." He reached out and wrapped his arms around her. "You want to go on this crazy ass ride with me, baby?"

She pulled back and looked in his face. The smile she gave him could have sent Torque down to his fucking knees. It was insane how he had done a complete one-eighty over this girl, changed how he felt about life, and actually wanted to give this shit a chance.

"This is crazy. You know that, right?"

She was still smiling and he couldn't help but smile back. "Don't I fucking know it, but I know in my gut it will be worth it." She didn't ask why he had changed so quickly, why his thoughts had done some kind of Mr. Hyde bullshit, she just accepted it, and wasn't that what trust was all about? Besides, Torque didn't know if he would have been able to give her an honest answer anyway. Shit, he had never felt anything like this, and at this point was hanging on tight and going with the flow. He leaned down and kissed her forehead, but the sound of someone clearing their throat broke up their little moment.

"Well isn't this all sweet and sentimental and shit." Pinkie leaned against the doorframe and narrowed her eyes at Delilah. Well fuck, he had totally forgotten about the Cherry, who had probably been standing in the hallway watching the whole scenario play out.

\*\*\*\*

"Ain't this some shit. I don't get to fuck Brack because he puts him in a bad mood, and now I'm in a bad mood because I didn't get what I wanted." Pinkie pushed off of the doorframe and took a step inside. Her heels clicked against the wood floor the closer she came. "I mean, what in the hell am I supposed to do now?" Delilah didn't miss the way she eyed Torque. "How about you and I go for a ride, big boy?" Pinkie grinned and flicked her eyes to Delilah.

Delilah stared at Pinkie and smiled. It was a bullshit expression, one that was all saccharine and shit, but hell, this bitch was about to go down. This had been a long time in coming. "Why don't you take your skank ass out of this room and continue until the front door hits you in your skinny ass."

The sound of Pinkie grinding her teeth sounded loud in the room. Good, she was getting to the bitch. "The only reason anyone keeps your uptight ass around is because you're Brack's bastard kid." Oh no, the hell she didn't just say that.

Delilah held her hand up to stop Torque from coming any closer, and the deep sound he made told her that he was just as pissed as she was. But this was her fight, and was at least four years in the making. "I may be, but the only reason they keep you around is because you are a fucking slut that sucks a bunch of bikers' dicks hoping one day you'll be an Old Lady Newsflash, none of them want your loose ass as anything more than a hole to fill."

Pinkie squeaked in outrage and lunged forward, but Delilah was ready. In fact, her entire body shook from the adrenaline pounding through her. Her right hand was already a fist by the time Pinkie was in hitting distance, and that was just what Delilah did. She swung out, connected with her boney ass face, and had the slut's whole body flipping to the side from the force of her punch. Pinkie fell to the ground, but not before she reached out and dragged her acrylic nails down Delilah's arm. She hissed out and covered the scratch marks with her hand. "You stupid bitch."

"No, you're the stupid bitch."

Pinkie pulled herself off the ground and ran a finger along her bottom lip that was split right open. "You think he's gonna want you when he can have ass like this?" She gestured to herself. "Not likely. You'll be the Old Lady that stays at home while he comes to the clubhouse to bang a hotter piece of ass."

Now it was Delilah's turn to lunge forward. Grabbing a chunk of the bleach-blonde's hair she ripped an extension right out, and grinned when Pinkie screamed. The sound of boots slamming down the hall pierced the anger Delilah felt, but no way was she letting her hold go. She yanked Pinkie forward and dragged her out of the room and down the hall. Ace and Vain moved out of her way with hands in the air, and when she reached the main floor where everyone was partying she stopped.

"Brack, tell this bitch to let me go."

Her father knitted his brows. "What's going on, Delilah?"

"No, Dad. This slut has had this a long time coming now." Pinkie gave another little shriek of outrage. She leaned in close to the Cherry's ear and said, "See, honey. No one has respect for a girl that doesn't care about anything but some deep dicking." With that she finished making her way toward the front door, pulled it open, and tossed her ass outside. Before she shut the door she turned around and addressed the members. "Do any of you want to claim this piece of shit as an Old Lady, or is everyone good with her ass getting banned from the clubhouse?" There was a collective silence, and then everyone murmured that they were not getting involved with female disputes. Good. She turned back to Pinkie, who was now standing and glaring at her with her hands on her hips. "Don't come back unless you want me to beat your ass again." She turned to one of the prospects. "Take her home."

Marson nodded and moved past Delilah.

She slammed the door closed and instantly felt more at ease. Everyone stared at her, and she thought maybe they'd bitch because she had overstepped some line, but in unison they threw their heads back and started laughing.

"Damn, Delilah. Didn't know you had that kind of spunk in you." Ace ruffled her hair and grinned down at her.

Vain pulled her to his side and patted her shoulder. "I was wondering when you'd finally get around to holding your own with her."

She elbowed him in the ribs and he grunted. Everyone moved to the bar for a round of shots, but she stayed back and saw Torque leaning against the wall. He had his shirt and cut back on, but there were some splatters of blood on the white tee from his busted lip. He pushed off the wall and moved toward her, and when he was right in front of her reached out and took hold of the back of her neck.

"Is it wrong to admit that you kicking Pinkie's ass turned me on?" Torque grinned.

Pinkie's words played through her head.

"What she said—" He cut her off with a firm shake of his head.

"If I wanted easy, loose pussy I would have gotten that and wouldn't have gone up against the club president for rights to have you to myself."

She knew this, and also knew that they could have easily voted on taking his patch. It was a slippery slope when a member went against the "rules", and she also knew that each chapter had different standards. He had risked a lot to make it known that she wasn't just a piece for him, but still she had seen brothers getting it on with a Cherry when their Old Lady was at home. That was not something she was going to stand, and she wanted to know upfront, and not when her heart was already too deep in the mix.

"Woman, you'll listen to me loud and clear. What I want is you, and only you. Maybe I didn't realize that until right now, but I sure as hell have been thinking about it, and trying to bury that shit deep down. I am not used to feeling these things, but I do know that I can't walk away from you or what we could have." He brushed his thumb along her cheekbone.

"Everyone is watching."

He shook his head and stared into her eyes. "I don't give a shit who is watching. Let them get a fucking eyeful. The important thing is that I would never fuck around on you. Ever, Delilah. There isn't any question about that, yeah?"

She swallowed the emotion down, and blocked out everything else aside from Torque and the words he was saying. "How would this work with you being a Nomad and on the road constantly? We'd never see each other." It took him several seconds to answer, but she didn't get the feeling that what he was going to say would suck.

"I don't know, baby. I have thought about settling down with a charter, this one in particular, but always pushed that back because I didn't want to be tied down."

"And now?" She held her breath.

"Well, I think there might be something worth settling down for. I can't guarantee I'll be easy to deal with. I'm stubborn and can be an asshole on the best of days, but I'm willing to try and do this…whatever this is." He grinned and cupped both of her cheeks in his big hands. "Besides, I saw a piece of property for sale right when I entered Rush Falls. Maybe that was a sign that I need to plant some roots, huh?"

"I think I'd like if you planted some roots, Torque."

He continued to rub his thumbs over her cheeks, and had this almost lost look on his face.

"What?"

"Noting. It's just that I could get so lost in you. Hell, I'm already halfway there."

Her heart hiccupped a little at his words.

"Either get a room or come over here and join us in a round of shots," Ace called out.

"Ain't no one getting a fucking room," Brack growled out right before he threw a shot back. He may have backed off a little, giving her the room she needed to see if what her and Torque had would last, but she knew he wouldn't be fully onboard with it. She was his little girl, and always would be. Maybe he thought she was making a mistake, but that was her mistake to make, and one she would have to learn from.

Torque took her hand and gave it a little squeeze. He led them over to the bar, and just like that the guys started bullshitting. This was her family, would always be her family, and she was damn lucky to be a part of it. If someone would have told her that she'd be standing here with Torque holding her hand, her dad and the others all standing around them not knocking his teeth out because of it, she would have called them all damn liars. Maybe she'd wake up and realize this was all one fucked-up dream, but until then she'd enjoy one hell of a ride.

**Jenika Snow** is the pseudonym of a mother, wife and nurse. She lives in the too hot northeast with her husband and their two daughters, and was able to have her dream come true in 2013 by writing full-time. She started writing at a very young age. Her first story consisted of a young girl who traveled to an exotic island and found a magical doll. That story has long since disappeared, but others have taken its place. Jenika loves to hear from readers, and encourages them to contact her and give their feedback.

For more information on other books by Jennika, visit her official website: JenikaSnow.com

## Also by Author

*A Beautiful Prison*

**Evernight Publishing**
*The Outlaw's Dirty Dancer*
*The Outlaw's Obsession*
*The Fighter's Girl*
*Her Tattooed Fighter*
*Hurts So Good*
*Bared for Her Bear*
*A Fox Between the Bear's Sheet*
*Fighting Dirty for His Girl*
*The Cougar's Timid Little Lynx*
*The Bear's Reluctant Wolf*
*A Kitty in the Lion's Den*
*A Lamb for the Bear's Appetite*
*Bear Naked and Bite Marks*
*Deep, Hard, and Rough*
*Breed Her*
*Giving it to the Bad Boy*
*Denying the Bad Boy*
*Sparrow's Flight*
*Lifting Tail for the Alpha*
*The First Time*
*A Virgin for Two Brothers*
*The Highest Bidder*
*The Bothers' Virgin Captive*
*One Night with the Billionaire*

*Under Two Billionaire Brothers*
*Dominated Their Virgin Sub*
*Tempting Her Best Friend's Father*
*Being with the Brothers Next Door*
*Seducing Her Brother's Best Friend*
*The Suit and His Switch Claim Their Sub*
*The Lion and the Lamb*
*Claiming What's Theirs*
*The Edge of Forever*
*Falling for Trouble*
*Playing with Fire*
*The Diary of Anna's Submission*
*The Taste of Blood*
*The Craving*
*The Chosen*
*Deliciously Wicked*
*Temptation Unveiled*
*Feral Cravings*
*Insatiable*
*Carnal*
*Lush*
*Savage*

# SCREWED

---

## BAD BOYS EROTIC ROMANCE

---

## SAM CRESCENT

# CHAPTER 1

"You're a fucking asshole."

Jesse Jenkins watched the woman he'd just fucked storm around the room. Tiffany was her name and she was well-known for fucking club men in the Demons MC. This was his room in the clubhouse and he'd be damned if he moved for the bitch. He also knew Tiffany was known by many motorcycle clubs, the other being the Hell's Charter a town over. Jesse hated the other bikers; they were fucking thieves.

"Whatever," he said, exhaling a ring of smoke up to the ceiling. What was it with women? One second they were all over you, wanting to suck your cock, and then when you told them the score, they got all bitchy.

"You really are an evil son of a bitch, aren't you?"

Why was she still fucking talking? Did she not know he hated women who constantly talked after fucking?

Stubbing out his cigarette, Jesse stared at the woman intent on giving him a headache. "Are you still fucking here?" he asked, wanting her out of his room and out of the club. Her pussy was great for the time he'd used her but now he wanted her out.

"I hate you. I can't believe I did this again."

"Tiffany, let's be clear, you'll always be in this position. No one wants you for an old lady. You're a fucking whore and you're only good for one thing — on your back with your legs spread.

She growled, threw an empty shot glass toward him and stormed out of his room. He heard laughter in the distance as she walked away.

"Jesse's pissed off another one." It had to be Spike talking. The other fucker didn't know how to keep his mouth fucking shut.

Staring at the broken glass, he rolled his eyes. He'd get one of the sweet butts to clear that shit away.

Grabbing his jacket from the back of the door, he put it on as he made his way down to the main club. Several men were already sipping coffee as he approached. "You look too fucking cheery," Ben said.

Nodding at the other men, Jesse took a seat and waited for his coffee. Leslie, one of the sweet butts — and a good screw — poured the coffee.

"Hey, sweetness, I don't suppose you'd take your sweet ass upstairs and clean up the glass Tiffany broke." Using his smoothest voice, Jesse tried to appeal to her kind heart.

"I'm not cleaning up after that whore," Leslie said.

Raising a brow, Jesse took a sip of the hot liquid.

"Come on, Jesse, you know what the women

think of other women," Spike said, interrupting the moment.

Jesse knew all about the jealousy going on between all the women within the club but they all had a certain standard for each other. Leslie was a club sweet butt as she didn't go to any other club whereas Tiffany wasn't held in the same regard. Tiffany would fuck anything with a cock and would never be allowed in on club business.

"Damn right. I'll clean your room for you but not because of her." Jesse watched her walk off, grabbing some cleaning supplies before calling out to the other women to help her clean his room.

"Man, you almost got fucked over and had to clean your own room." Spike chuckled, spilling coffee over the counter.

"Shut the fuck up. You know Tiffany's got a nice pussy and mouth. I was in the mood for ease and she's that kind of woman." Shaking his head, Jesse stepped away from the counter. He moved toward the front door, intent on getting out of the building and into the fresh morning air. It was icy cold out but he liked the feel of the chill.

At thirty years old he loved life. Becoming a member of Demons was the best thing that had ever happened to him. The club life, the women, the feel of his bike between his thighs were the best feelings in the world. He sipped some coffee before lighting up his cigarette and turned to stare at the clubhouse that was also his home.

He owned an apartment in town but most of his life was in this one building. No women went back to his place. This is where his life would remain.

"I thought I'd find you out here. You're the only man I know who likes to freeze your balls off first thing in the morning." Charley, Demons president and friend joined him.

"What can I say? I love to keep my junk cool." Chuckling, Jesse took a long drag on his cigarette. "What brings you out this early? Last time I checked you were balls deep in your wife."

"She's back home taking care of the kids. It's a good thing they're not at the clubhouse today."

"Why?" Sometimes the wives and kids would stop by and have a party or some fun but when real business needed to be dealt with, they stayed away.

"We've got a problem, Jesse. One of our boys fucked up and paid the price. Now I need to know what the fuck is going on." Frowning, he stared at Charley. "We've got church."

Pouring the coffee on the ground as he no longer wanted it, Jesse followed behind Charley. The club was empty apart from some women lazing around. Several women eyed him up and down.

Shaking his head, he closed the door, and took a seat around the table.

"I've got some bad news." Charley looked around the whole table before talking again. "Junior is fucking dead."

"What?" Spike asked.

"How the fuck did this happen?" Another of the club men demanded to know.

"He was partying with those Hell's Charter guys. It's the only way they'd get close to him." This came from Spike again.

The boys shouted, cursed, and talked reasons as

to why one of their own got whacked.

"I'm not going to spend time thinking about why it happened. Junior's dead and now we've got to deal with the consequences. His body was a fucking mess." Charley rubbed a hand over his face.

"He was tortured?" Jesse asked.

"Yeah, he was tortured, and I'm guessing he gave some shit up. We don't know what he gave up but I'm not taking the risk." Leaning forward, he assessed the group before turning his gaze on Jesse. "Which is why I'm about to ask you for a favor."

Tensing, Jesse waited for what was about to come his way. He knew there was a chance he wasn't going to like it.

"You're the only person we know who can get close to this woman and get the information we need."

A picture of a chestnut-haired fat girl stared at him. Well, she wasn't fat, just not slender. She wore a pair of jeans and a shirt that were clearly three times too big for her. He noticed she wasn't smiling at all. In fact, she looked sad as she talked to someone.

"This is the Piper Rix. She's the daughter of John, the President of the Hell's Charter. They keep her close and she's one of the few women who knows club business."

"You want me to infiltrate the Hell's Charter?" Jesse asked, disgusted.

"No, we want you to get into her pants and find out everything she knew about Junior."

Laughing, Jesse lifted the photo and couldn't help the kick in the gut he got. There was something about the woman in the picture that struck him to the core. No, he wasn't going to do it.

"I doubt she knows anything about Junior." Throwing the picture onto the desk, he stared at Charley.

"She knows everything about the club. Her father adores her and never allows her to go too far from home." Charley picked up the picture. "I know she's not much to look at but we need you to do this."

"They've not attacked us, have they?" Jesse asked, sitting back.

"No, and I want to keep it that way. I want them to stay out of our business and we stay out of theirs. You will do this or I'll kick your ass out of my club." Charley made the threat while smiling.

"Fine, what do you want me to do?"

"She spends mornings reading at this coffee shop." Charley pulled another picture out of a file and pointed. "Go there tomorrow morning. Don't be interested in the club life. Be interested in her. You'll also need to use your apartment."

"What the fuck?"

"No women. We need you to get her to fall in love with you. You'll not be coming here and you won't be having any women. Also, we've put you down for work at Western's mechanic shop. He's got a place for you."

Staring at his boss, Jesse wondered if it was some kind of prank.

"We're counting on you, Jesse."

Great, there was nothing he could do or say. Picking up the picture, he stared at the woman he was about to get to fall in love with him. Crap, he'd never tried with a woman before. How was he going to make this work?

\*\*\*\*

Piper Rix ordered her coffee and croissant before sitting in the corner booth near the window. She sat in the back to watch people pass her by in between reading the latest romance her father had bought her. It was kind of embarrassing when her father bought her romance books to pass the time. This was his way of getting her out of the clubhouse and into normal life. He never trusted anyone around her. At twenty-two years old she'd never been on a real date.

For prom she found out her father had organized her date. The whole night had been horrible knowing the man with her was only there for money and to win her father's favor. John Rix meant well and she never said a word to him that she knew.

She was a virgin, as she didn't trust men. Most of the men she did know were introduced by her father, and she knew they were only after something from him.

The waitress brought over her coffee and food. Piper smiled her thanks, opened up her book and started to read. Her time alone would go by easier if she read. At twelve, one of the boy's would pick her up to take her back to the Hell's Charter clubhouse.

Sipping her coffee, she added a little sugar to get it just right.

Turning the page, she ignored someone clearing their throat. No one ever approached her and she figured it wouldn't change today.

"Excuse me?" Someone tapped her shoulder.

Looking up she stared into intense blue eyes that smiled down at her. His blond hair was tied behind the back of his neck. She saw the ink that swirled around his neck and clearly went down his arms.

When she realized the man was talking to her, she licked her lips and responded.

"Can I help you?" she asked, feeling her cheeks heat.

"Is this seat taken?"

Frowning, she stared around the coffee shop to see plenty of seats available. But she'd never been rude in her life and she wasn't going to start now.

"Erm, I'll be done soon and you can have this table." Rubbing her temple, she opened her book to start reading again, hoping he'd leave.

He took a seat, pulling out a newspaper. She stared at him, completely shocked. His legs brushed her knees and she sat up straighter to stop contact.

"I didn't offer you a seat." Saying the words made her feel rude.

"I'm Jesse, and this is where I want to sit." He offered her a hand, offering no apology. For several seconds she debated arguing with him then thought better of it. She hated causing scenes and the place was full with customers.

Shaking it, Piper smiled. "Piper."

"I heard this was an awesome coffee shop. I can't drink coffee without company and you looked in need of some." He leaned forward on his elbows. His smile made her heart flutter as all of his attention was directed at her.

"I, er, I never have company."

"It's so cold outside and everyone else looks busy. What book are you reading?" he asked.

This had to be the single weirdest experience of her life. She lifted the book up for him to see, Jesse read the title and nodded.

"Cool. So, do you come here often?"

She'd barely spoken and Piper was starting to get suspicious. "Do you know John Rix?"

Jesse leaned back, his gaze on hers. His brows furrowed close as he stared at her chest. Glancing down, she saw her shirt gapped open, showing a lot of cleavage. She tugged the shirt together before looking back at him.

"That's a shame. I really enjoyed the view."

Her cheeks must be hotter than the sun. Crap, what the hell was this guy doing to her?

"No, I don't know a John Rix." He stopped as the waitress put down a mug of coffee with a plate of sandwiches.

Piper saw the waitress place her number underneath the plate.

"I don't think so, sweetheart," Jesse said, handing back the card. "I'm not interested."

She watched the waitress storm off, calling Jesse a chubby chaser.

"You didn't have to do that," she said "I wouldn't take offense. She's a beautiful woman."

Jesse stared at her without saying a word for several seconds.

"I'm happy staring at the beautiful woman in front of me. No, I don't know John Rix and I'd like to take you out on a date."

"You don't know me."

"I watched you walk here. Why do you keep your head down? Why are you here alone? Do you have a man at home?" His questions kept coming her way.

Flustered, she picked up her cold coffee and took a sip. "You're asking a lot of questions."

"I'm getting to know you. How can we get to know each other without asking questions?"

"We don't." Biting her lip she glanced down at her book, wishing he would disappear.

"You're going to make it difficult for me to know you?"

Glancing up, she stared at him. "I come here to enjoy some coffee and to have something to eat. I'm not interested in whatever you're trying to do."

He sat back staring at her. "Then you're going to have to get used to it, baby. I'm not giving up."

Hearing the sound of a motorcycle, she looked out of the window to see her father's vice president pulling up near the window. Dale was a good man but he wasn't known for his patience.

"I'm done for the day." Piper closed her book and climbed out of her seat. She took out some bills out of her pocket and left. She felt his eyes on her as she left.

Trying her best to ignore him, she grabbed the helmet Dale offered. "What's wrong with you, princess?"

"Nothing, I'm fine."

She didn't look toward the window. Climbing on the back of the bike, she wrapped her arms around his waist and together they drove off toward the clubhouse.

The drive to the clubhouse didn't take long at all. Piper gave the helmet back to Dale before making her way into the building. She was frozen to the core.

"Honey, how was your trip?" John asked, coming out of his office.

"Good." She opened her mouth to ask him about the guy at the coffee shop, then she simply smiled. If he employed someone to sit with her during those days, she didn't want to know the answer.

The following week she'd all but forgotten about the man who'd joined her for coffee. She ordered her coffee and a sandwich before sitting down to start to read her book.

"I see you have the same table again," Jesse said, sitting down without asking permission first.

"Are you following me?" she asked, sitting back.

"Yes." He put the newspaper on the table staring at her the whole time. "I wanted to make sure you came here. I only watched you from outside."

A thrill shot through her body at his admission. "You were watching me?"

She'd never had a man watch her before or pay any kind of attention to her. Piper hated the fact she liked it. How pathetic was she? A virgin begging for attention.

"Yes, I like watching you. Do you only come here Friday mornings?" he asked.

"No, I come here Mondays as well. I only have coffee then."

Would it hurt getting to know the man who was looking back at her? His gaze wandered down her body and she felt owned by him. The possession wasn't something she was used to.

"Great."

The waitress placed their orders on the table before leaving again.

"What is your game?" she asked. Growing up around the men of the Hell's Charter gave her good insight to the male psyche. She knew a lot of men only did certain things for attention.

"No game at all. You must have dated some serious rats to be this dubious about men."

She tore open two packets of sugar and poured them into her coffee. She probably should steer clear of sugar to lose some weight but she'd grown tired of the never-ending battle. John always got pissed when he found out she was dieting. The New Year would be upon them in no time and she vowed to lose weight then.

"You've gone all quiet on me," he said, pulling her out of her thoughts.

"Look, I just want to have coffee. I don't want to make any commitments or even understand why you're interested in me." Licking her lips, she tried to keep her thoughts on her words. "Please, stop with the flattery. I don't know why you're here and I don't care."

"Wow, you really know how to shoot a guy

down." Jesse looked around him and smiled. "You're a challenge. I'm always up for one."

She shook her head and couldn't help but smile. Piper looked forward to seeing more of him, especially if he wasn't there at her father's demand.

# CHAPTER TWO

For three weeks Jesse went to the coffee shop twice a week. A total of six meetings including the two prior, which meant eight in total and he still wasn't close to finding out anything about the Hell's Charter—or even about Piper Rix. She kept her feelings close to her chest. There were flashes of emotion that crossed her face but before he got a read on her, they disappeared. He hated the lack of reading her more than anything else.

Never in all of his life had he found wooing a woman so difficult. Piper was reserved around him. He got her to smile at least. But getting her to smile was entirely different than her telling him club secrets.

He ran his fingers through his hair for something to do with his hands. His nerves were totally fried when it came to Piper. Fuck, three weeks without getting his dick wet from one of the club whores and sitting across from a sexy woman was starting to wear thin. When Piper leaned forward or moved in such a way he got a good glimpse of the pale flesh of her breasts, he wanted to bury his head against those mounds to lick and suck her nipples. Her nipples would be large and he'd spend plenty of time on each bud.

He was getting hard thinking about the time he'd spend fucking her.

A knock at his door brought him out of his plan. He lit a cigarette and checked who stood in front of his door before he opened it.

"I thought I wasn't allowed near the club?" he stated, letting Charley inside

"So? This is an apartment building, genius. I could be visiting anyone."

They walked toward the sitting room. Jesse differed to the kitchen to grab a beer from the fridge. He threw Charley a cool beer then took a seat across from him.

"What's the news?" Charley asked.

"Nothing new. Bitch is a hard nut to break." Jesse took a long inhale on his cigarette. He didn't want to let on that he liked her. Crap, thinking about Piper had heat rushing to his cock making him rock hard. There was no way he'd be able to handle getting a hard-on with his boss seeing.

"Come on, Jesse, I know you. You've had a month of working the charm. What's taking so long? We need to know what Junior gave up or we're all fucked," Charley said. "The Hell's Charter and the Demons have an understanding not to fuck with each other's business. If Junior was a fucking snitch and working elsewhere besides with us, then I understand why they offed him but I need to make sure."

"What more do you want from me? I'm drinking coffee and talking. She's got tighter lips than a fucking virgin." Thinking about Piper's plump lips made Jesse want to kiss her over and over. Great, he was turning into a fucking pussy who thought about kissing, romance, and other shit.

"You've not gotten fucking inventive? Did I say you had to woo her at the fucking coffee shop? How are you going to screw her there? For fuck's sake, Jesse, I thought you had some fucking brains to you."

"I do have brains." He'd just not thought about leaving the coffee shop. Wasting three weeks hadn't been his idea of fun.

"All the boys are tense waiting for you to come through. I suggest you pull your finger out and start wooing this girl." Charley stood, heading toward the door. At the last minute he stopped and turned around. "Be careful with this girl. I've heard she's a sweetheart."

"How am I supposed to do that when you want me to fuck her for information?" Jesse asked, following close behind.

"Don't make any fucking promises you can't keep? Only promise and give her what you're prepared for."

Charley walked out. Kicking the door closed, Jesse stubbed his cigarette out before heading out. He'd hired one of his boys to follow her over the last few weeks. He checked the time. She'd be shopping at the supermarket right now. It was time to step up his wooing and get this shit over with. Grabbing his jacket from the back of the door, he hated the fact he couldn't wear his leathers. Since he'd taken the job of dealing with Piper Rix, he'd put all of his leather cuts into his safe. Anything relating him to the Demons he'd gotten rid of. What he hated most was not being able to ride his bike. He'd spent years working on his pride and joy, replacing the engine then getting the paint work done. Before joining the Demons he'd qualified as a mechanic. He loved working with machines but he loved working for Charley more.

Firing up the engine in his truck, he pulled out of the lot, heading toward the supermarket out of town. He spotted Piper's car instantly. It was a shit make and model and something women would drive. He learned she only drove it on very rare occasions and her father preferred her to be escorted by one of the club. Her father was very protective of her. Parking beside her, he headed into the supermarket. Jesse, with basket in hand, started to put groceries inside. He couldn't freak her out by just showing up looking like a stalker.

He kept an eye on the people around him. Jesse spotted her around the meat counter looking at a large piece of beef.

"Do you think that will serve thirty?" Piper asked. "I've got a Sunday lunch and the whole family is going to be there."

"I'd recommend a second, miss."

"Okay, I'll take the two." She was looking down at her list, nibbling her lip as she crossed off another item.

The guy tried to talk to her some more. Jesse stayed back to see what she'd do. Piper smiled at him, wished him a good day then walked away. She had no idea how beautiful she was.

Following behind her, he saw the aisle she went down. Going around, he walked toward her from the opposite direction.

She was bent down looking at some chocolate.

When she stood, he bumped into her, reaching out to stop her from falling. He wrapped his arms around her waist, pulling her in close.

"I'm so sorry," he said, staring down into her eyes.

"Jesse, coffee shop guy." She chuckled. Caressing her waist, Jesse really didn't want to let her go. "Are you following me around?" Piper took a step back giving him no choice other than to release her.

"No." Lifting up his basket of goods to show her, he returned the smile. "I'm out shopping. Being a single guy I've got no choice but to keep myself supplied. You?"

"Shopping for the family."

"Pretty big family." He eyed the steaks, knowing how many she cooked for.

"Yeah, all my dad's boys are going to be there. They love their steak and potatoes. What about you? Would you like an invite or something?"

Staring into her eyes, Jesse knew that's what she was waiting for. She truly believed he was after a shot in the Hell's Charter. "Nah, I'd rather spend time with you than getting to know your family." He meant the words he spoke.

"Really?" she asked. Piper looked into his basket and frowned. "What are you making?"

He checked out what he'd put inside his basket, a bag of apples, four tins of tuna, a can opener and some peppers. The combination alone made him feel sick.

"Erm, a stir fry."

She giggled. "Come on. I can get you the right stuff for a stir fry." Piper linked arms with him and together they made their way through the supermarket.

For several minutes Jesse forgot about the club life and everything else. Piper took his attention away, making him feel alive. The way he felt in her company was similar to the way he felt on a bike.

"I promise you, chicken stir fry with fresh vegetables and the right sauces is much better than that pre-packed stuff you can buy. Better for you too." She paid for her shopping, waiting for him.

They headed out together.

"Where are you parked?" she asked.

"Over there."

"You're right beside me."

"Wow, I must be lucky," he said, smiling. His gut tightened at the lies he was spinning. All of a sudden the real reason he was pursuing her invaded his thoughts.

"What's the matter?"

"Nothing. Do you want to come to my place? You can bring your shopping and I'll put it in my fridge to keep. We could have some dinner, talk, get to know each other without coffee present."

He just created the perfect opening to get her alone away from prying eyes.

\*\*\*\*

The smile froze on her lips. Piper had so much fun shopping with him. She shouldn't be giving him the time of day. Was he a stalker? How did he seem to know everything about her?

*Stop it, Piper.*

She always doubted everyone, especially men. Glancing over at the supermarket, she nibbled her lip trying to think about his question.

"I promise, chicken stir fry is the only thing on the menu. I won't be chopping you up or anything." She saw his cheeks heat as he looked away.

Piper laughed. "I'd love to have some food with you."

"Excellent. Do you want to follow me?"

"Yes, I'm just going to make a call and then I'll be with you." She quickly put the bags into her car then climbed into the front seat. Her hands were shaking as she picked up her cell phone.

"Hey, honey, what's the matter?" John asked.

"Dad, I'm going to be a bit longer. I'm going to a friend's for dinner."

"A friend?"

"Yeah, someone I've met recently. You wouldn't know...him." She hit her head wishing she'd not let the "him" out of the bag.

"Him?"

"No, please, don't make a big deal out of this. Are you good to get dinner yourself? I've got everything for Sunday."

He tried to talk her out of going. Piper found herself wanting to go. Jesse gave her a thrill that she'd never experienced in her life.

*I deserve a thrill.*

"Be careful, honey. Let us know when you're on the road."

He wasn't happy but she didn't care. "I will."

She disconnected the call and waved at Jesse, who laughed. Following close behind him, Piper felt her nerves starting to pick up. What the hell was she doing?

"Just keep driving. You can do this, Piper. It's only dinner. Nothing else." She parked alongside him, surprised when he helped her with shopping before grabbing his own.

Neither of them spoke on the way up to the apartment.

Her hands were sweaty and she stood behind him while he opened the door. "Welcome to my home."

The scent of cigarette smoke was in the air with a hint of pine.

"Sorry, I smoke." He walked to the window, opening it up.

"No, it's fine. I don't smoke but all of my dad's boys do. Don't worry about it. Can I put this beef in the fridge? I don't want it to spoil."

"Sure. Put it in here."

He opened the fridge and she placed the beef inside, then stood to look at him.

"Do you want to get started on the chicken?" Her stomach rumbled and she coughed, trying to cover up the sound.

"I'm starving. If you don't mind we can cook, eat, then watch a movie," he said, emptying the bags onto the counter.

"Watch out." He'd tipped the contents of the bags onto the counter and a bottle of soy sauce fell off the counter onto the floor. She picked it up, seeing the bottle survived. "No, we're good. Soy is crucial in a stir fry."

Handing him the bottle, she helped him place the ingredients out.

"Right, I've never made a stir fry in my life," he said.

Chuckling, she nudged him out of the way. "Good for you, I have."

She searched his kitchen, finding a wok, a chopping board, and knife. Piper set him to work cutting vegetables as she marinated the chicken.

"Don't you have a wife or girlfriend to do this for you?" she asked, wondering if she heard wrong back in the grocery store. There was no way this man was single.

"Baby, if I had a woman in my life I wouldn't be trying to get you around to my place."

Excitement zipped through her veins. Ignoring the excitement, she turned on the heat. His arm brushed against hers. "Relax, Piper. I'm not going to hurt you. I promise you're safe with me."

"I'm fine."

How could she tell him she wasn't used to men flirting with her? Was he flirting with her? She didn't even know what he was trying to do.

For the next thirty minutes she worked on the stir fry, mixing everything together as she instructed Jesse to add ingredients. The scents of garlic, ginger, and chili were amazing. Finally, she added some pre-cooked noodles before serving it into two bowls.

"This smells amazing," Jesse said, hovering over. She watched him take a fork and dive in, burning his mouth. "Ow, I tell you, baby, this is fucking delicious."

She stared at the ink around his neck. Without his jacket on and wearing a short-sleeved T-shirt, she was able to see the ink up his arms.

"Are you part of a group or something?" she asked.

"Or something."

Jesse handed her a bowl and she followed him back through to the sitting room. His apartment was nice and clean. "Sit there," he said, pointing to the end of the sofa.

Sitting down, she waited for him to sit then dove into her food. She was so hungry and felt embarrassed by how hungry she actually was.

"I love a woman who knows how to eat."

"What?" She paused with the fork on her lips.

"Nowadays women are all worrying about being the perfect size and ordering a salad. We only have this life once and most people waste it by restraining themselves. I'd rather be on a date with a woman who likes to eat." His smile made her heart pound.

Besides family gatherings, Piper made every effort to never eat in front of other people. "Erm, great I guess."

She ate in silence, listening to Jesse moan.

"Woman, you've got to marry me," he said.

There were times when he spoke that she wondered if he was part of a motorcycle club similar to her father's. The men she grew up with didn't keep their emotions in check. They always spoke without a filter.

Ignoring his words, she finished her food, wishing the unease would disappear. When they were finished she helped him do the dishes, then went toward the fridge. "It's been lovely but I need to head out." She turned to see Jesse standing close.

"Stay." His hand rested beside her head. "We'll watch a movie and have some fun."

Fingers stroked through her hair and Piper felt a pulse between her thighs. She didn't know what to do or say.

"What are you doing?" she asked.

"Nothing you don't want. Can you feel it, Piper?"

She shook her head even as her nipples tightened, pressing against the loose shirt she wore. She always wore clothing bigger than her shape as she hated trying to fit her figure into any clothes.

"A movie?" Her voice was high pitched.

"Yes, a movie."

"Okay."

He left the room, grabbing a movie from his bedroom.

*Come on, Piper, you can do this. One movie and then you're out of here.*

Running her sweaty palms down her thighs, she licked her lips and then tucked some hair behind her ear. This was the first time she'd spent any length of time with a man who wasn't a Hell's Charter member.

Jesse placed the DVD inside the player, then took a seat beside her.

He sat so close that she felt his body heat radiating.

*Stop losing your mind. Be sane, Piper.*

The movie started and she found herself relaxing when she saw it was some kind of racing movie.

All too soon that relaxation disappeared as Jesse leaned in close, caressing her hair. She tensed, not knowing what to expect.

"Relax, Piper."

His voice was hypnotic. She closed her eyes and let out a moan. His fingers were stroking her neck, which felt like the most pleasure she'd ever had.

"I'm here, baby." He'd moved closer in the last few seconds.

Turning her head to look at him, she was struck by how handsome he was, tattoos and all. "I thought we were watching a movie."

"We were, and then I couldn't help but touch you. Your skin is so soft." His fingers glided over her cheek. "I want to kiss you, Piper."

The closer he got the more she panicked. She'd never kissed anyone in her life.

Jesse's lips were on hers before she got the chance to panic. She opened her lips and he plundered, stroking inside. The kiss deepened and his hands were stroking all over her body, building an inferno within her.

Heat pooled between her thighs. Her stomach knotted and her nipples were so tight they hurt.

An unbearable ache started and Jesse was the cause. She felt his fingers gliding down until he stopped, cupping her breast.

No, she couldn't do this. Jerking away, she stood, to get away from him. Her breathing was ragged.

"I can't do this," she said, stepping away.

Escape was all she thought about.

"What? I felt you, Piper. You were with me."

She moved to the fridge, grabbing her shopping, then whirled around to face him. "I've never done anything like this. This was only supposed to be food and a movie. I've never even been on a date." Her words were running away from her.

Slapping a hand against her lips, she headed toward the door wishing the floor would open up to swallow her whole.

"Are you trying to tell me you're a fucking virgin?"

She froze, turning to look at him in horror. No one knew her secret and hearing him mock her current status hurt.

"Shit, you are. I'm sorry."

"Forget it. This was a mistake. It was all a mistake." She charged out of his apartment. Once outside, Piper spotted her car, climbed inside and was out of there.

# CHAPTER THREE

Jesse threw the vase he'd been given by a neighbor across his apartment. Fuck, his plans were screwing up left and right. He'd never taken a fucking virgin and was proud of himself for never getting mixed up with them. Virgins were females with expectations. He didn't do relationships and that was what a virgin expected.

"Fuck." Shouting the curse out failed to help his anger.

He grabbed his cell phone and dialed Charley's number.

"Do you have any news for me?" Charley asked.

"No. There's a problem. She's a fucking virgin, Charley. How the fuck can I screw the information out of a fucking virgin? She doesn't deserve this shit."

He hated to admit it but he'd grown to like her. She wasn't like any other woman he'd ever met. Women who grew up in the lifestyle rarely held any sense of innocence.

Piper wasn't really in the lifestyle. Her father was the club president while she was only his daughter.

"Then you're going to have to keep it up before you get rid of her. We need this information and I'd hoped we could get what we needed without hurting the poor girl. I can't think of anyone better to take her virginity. Give her body a party, Jesse. When you're done I won't ask anything else from you."

"I can't do this." Jesse gritted his teeth as he spoke.

"We all do our shit for the club. Do you expect the boys to be happy with looking over their shoulders every time they leave? I hate to bring the girl in but this has played out of our hands. Give me a call when you know more."

The line disconnected. Hating his president and the club, he threw the cell phone across the room. He needed to clear his head. He slammed out of the apartment, holding onto his jacket as he left. Jesse took the truck to the mechanic shop where he'd been told to work.

Western was working under the hood of a car as he pulled in. "I didn't expect you to be here at all." The mechanic wiped his hands on the grease cloth as he walked toward Jesse.

"I need to work on something. I've got to clear my head and I can't do that on my bike. You got anything for me to work on?" Pocketing his keys, he followed Western to a rundown rust bucket in need of several *years* of TLC.

"Will this do?" Western asked.

"Sure."

For the next few hours he worked on the rust bucket, wishing there was something more he could come up when it came to the problem at hand. Piper was a virgin and he knew all about fucking.

*Don't back down now. You've got to keep this up.*

Working on the car he cleared his thoughts seeing the problem had nothing to do with Piper. He needed to stop thinking about her as a job. There was where his conflict lay. With him seeing Piper as a job, something he needed to deal with, he lost all sense of seduction and need.

Blocking all thoughts of the job and task from his mind, Jesse allowed himself to simply think about Piper as a woman, a sexy, full, desirable woman. He'd gotten the chance to feel her full, rounded tits. They filled his hands perfectly. Her nipples were large and would fill his mouth as he sucked.

Every thought turned him on. Piper was a sexy woman and one he'd love to fuck in a heartbeat. He wondered what she'd look like when he brought her to climax. Jesse knew he could make her blossom underneath him.

No, his wooing wasn't over. In fact, it was only just beginning.

Smiling, feeling happier than he had in over four weeks, he delved into the project of the rusty car. He didn't care about anything else other than his plans of getting Piper on his side.

The following Monday he stood outside the coffee shop waiting for her to approach. Her head was bowed and when she got closer, he grabbed her arm tugging her away.

"Hey, what the hell are you doing?" she asked.

"We're going to have some time away from the

fucking coffee shop." Bundling her into the passenger side of the truck, he walked around to the driver's side.

"This is kidnapping. Do you have any idea who my father is?" she asked.

"No, and I don't give a fuck." He lied easily. Reaching across the truck, he held onto her neck, drawing her in close. Slamming his lips down onto hers he silenced her with a kiss.

She gasped, opening up for him to deepen it.

"Now, we're going to go out and have some fun. You're not allowed to doubt me or throw shit out that doesn't exist. Are we clear?" he asked.

"You're acting like someone crazy. What's going on?"

"I'm not giving you chance to read or do anything." He started up the truck. Jesse checked to make sure the road was clear before pulling out of the town square and headed out toward the nature park ten miles out.

For the first five minutes of their journey she was silent then she started to speak. He'd decided to give her the time and space she needed to get herself together.

"I'm sorry about the other day. It was foolish of me." Her hands were rubbing down her thighs.

"You were being honest with me." Taking hold of her hand, he kept on driving. "Don't ever be embarrassed to admit the truth."

"Are you sure?"

"Baby, you're a virgin, so what? I'm not around you for that." He no longer considered the words he spoke a lie.

"This is humiliating."

"How have you remained untouched?" he asked, keeping his eyes on the road. The thought of no other man knowing her body made him hard as rock. He'd take her to heights she never even knew existed.

"It's hard to trust anyone with who my father is. He's the president of the Hell's Charter. Have you heard of it?"

"No, I can't say that I have." Now he felt uncomfortable.

"Well, a lot of the guys are always there to see my father, trying to impress him. Let's just say I learned a man paying me attention hasn't always been innocent."

Gritting his teeth, Jesse couldn't help the anger. With the Demons no one used a woman to get into the club.

"I'm sorry you've had to deal with shit like that." Parking the truck, he turned the ignition off. Climbing out of the truck, he went to her side before she got chance to climb out. "This is about fun. No doubts, no crap. Just you and me, got it?" he asked.

"I got it." He didn't have a clue what he was doing. He locked up his truck and they started walking. The cold winter air gripped them and he wished he'd picked something else to do.

"What are we doing here?" she asked, shivering.

"I want to spend time with you but being in that blasted coffee shop is like being in a fucking nunnery. You hide from me, Piper. I'm tired of you hiding."

"You think getting me to freeze to death would be better?" She rubbed her hands together.

Wrapping his arms around her waist, he pulled her back against him. "Then we can share body heat," he whispered against her ear, and together they walked around the nature reserve. Jesse took his time, holding her close. She smelled lovely and lemony.

"Why did you bring me out here?" she asked.

"I want you, Piper." He held her tight, refusing to let her go.

"I don't believe you." She was tense in his arms. He wanted her to relax, to know what true desire really was.

Pressing his aching cock against her ass, he tugged her back. "You feel that?" She nodded. "I fucking ache for you, baby. I want to feel you underneath me, taking my cock."

"Jesse." She jerked but he kept a hold on her.

"Listen to me, Piper." He looked around, checking to make sure no one was watching. Gliding his hands up her body, he cupped her tits through the thin jacket she wore. He'd take her back to the truck very soon to warm up. "I want to fuck you, baby. I've been imagining you for a long time underneath me."

"We barely know each other." She was tense but he needed to get this out in the open.

"Our bodies don't need to know each other for longer. Is your pussy wet for me? Do you want me as badly as I want you?"

He turned her to face him, staring into her shocked face.

Her mouth opened then closed.

"It's all right. I'm not expecting you to answer." Cupping her face, he stared into her eyes.

"What do you want?" she asked.

"This Friday, if you want to explore this, then meet me outside of the coffee shop. Don't bring a book and I promise you, Piper, you won't regret giving yourself to me."

Jesse claimed her lips, cupping her ass and drawing her close to him. "I'm going to fuck you so hard. This Friday."

He didn't give her chance to dispute him as he led her back to the truck.

"If I don't want to?"

"Then you come with a book and I'll see it in your hand." Jesse hoped for his own sanity that she wanted him. This was no longer about his club but about himself.

\*\*\*\*

On Friday, Piper stared at her reflection wishing she could find something that would finally make up her mind. Over the last week she'd changed her mind over a dozen times. One moment she was going with Jesse on Friday then the next moment she wasn't.

"It doesn't matter," she said.

"What's gotten into you?" her father asked, walking by her bedroom door. She was at the Hell's Charter clubhouse.

"Nothing, Dad. I'm fine."

John stared at her for several moments. He walked inside her room. "Are you sure everything is fine? You've not been right since this boyfriend of yours came onto the scene."

"He's not my boyfriend. Only a friend."

*A friend who wants to fuck me.*

Averting her gaze, she grabbed her bag from the bed.

"Only a friend? Does he know about the club?" John asked, standing beside her.

"He doesn't seem to. Jesse hasn't asked about you. In fact, he's the first man who talks to me about everything *but* club business." Biting her lip, she stared down at the floor.

"What's going on, Piper? The boys have commented about your withdrawal from them." He tucked some of her hair behind her ear.

"Nothing is going on. I promise. It's woman stuff. That time of the month and all that." She crossed her fingers behind her back hoping he'd back off.

"Woman things?" John wrinkled his nose. "Okay, honey. I'll tell the boys to back off. They know better than to get mixed up with women during that trying time."

It took every ounce of will power not to burst out laughing.

"Thanks, Dad. I'm out for the day. Do you have everything under control here? I finished the books and I've also dealt with that crap Junior left you as well." She walked to her desk, handing him back the file John asked her to prepare.

"I really shouldn't involve you in club business," John said, taking the folder from her.

"No matter. I've got to earn my keep and this is

what you'd do if I'd been a boy. I'm not a rider but I can keep your business in working order. Bye, Dad." She kissed John on the cheek, heading out of the door. Stopping, she turned to look at him. "What happened to Junior? He's not been around here lately."

"Business, baby."

Smiling, she gave him a wave, heading out toward the coffee shop. She'd argued with her father about walking today rather than riding. Piper didn't want any of the men asking questions. The romance book she'd been reading was back at home. Looking up as she neared the coffee shop she saw Jesse, smoking a cigarette, leaning against the brick wall.

He really was a handsome man, sexy and dangerous at the same time.

"You came," he said.

"Yeah, I came." Glancing at the spot where she usually sat, Piper waited for him to speak.

"Did you bring your book?" he asked.

She shook her head. Words failed her in that moment.

"Do you want to come home with me?"

Piper wanted to get rid of her virginity. Jesse looked like the kind of man who'd give a woman pleasure.

"Yes, I want to go home with you," she said.

"Follow me." He took her hand once again leading her toward his truck. He helped her inside before taking his position beside her.

Her hands were sweaty again. Staring at everyone going about their business, she wondered if they knew what she was about to do.

Sex, she was about to go and have sex.

Heart pounding, she squeezed her thighs together to try to stem her arousal. Neither of them spoke as they made their way toward his apartment. He parked the truck and together they made their way up to his door.

Did he feel nervous about what they were about to do? She doubted it.

Once inside with the door closed, Jesse removed her coat.

His arms were around her, holding her close. Resting her head against his shoulder, she heard their breathing.

"Do you want this?" he asked.

"I'm here."

"Being here and wanting to be here are two different things." He spun her around to face him.

"Yes, I want to be here."

He took her further into the room. The curtains were still open but looking outside she saw no one would see them.

"You're so beautiful," he said, sinking his fingers into her hair.

"You don't have to say things like that."

"Like what?"

"Things like I'm beautiful. I'm here, Jesse."

His fingers tightened in her hair making her gasp. The sharp bite of pain turned her on, shocking her to her core.

"I'm not saying shit to get in your pants. This is who I am. I've been playing the nice guy for you. It's time to show you who I really am."

She really wanted to see the real him.

Jesse's free hand touched her between the thighs. Gasping, she tensed up at the blunt contact. He didn't hurt her, simply placed his hand on top of her clothing. Her coat was long gone; he'd taken care of that.

"You're mine. Today, tomorrow, you're not going anywhere," he said.

"I'll have to call home. Tell them not to come and get me."

"You've got a car. Why do you always get picked up?" Jesse asked.

"My dad is overprotective. I had to argue to walk to the coffee shop. He worries, but I don't mind the company."

"I don't care. I've got to fucking taste you." Jesse claimed her lips, stopping all thoughts. She opened to him, meeting his tongue with her own. Wrapping her arms around his neck, she held onto him. Her legs were like jelly against his onslaught of passion.

Passion, fuck, she wasn't in some kind of romance book.

"Are you wet for me?" he asked, breaking the kiss.

"Yes, I think so."

He went to his knees in front of her. The jeans she wore were suddenly gone, followed by her panties. In quick time he stood, removing her shirt and bra. She stared down at her body, trying to cover herself.

"No, you don't get to hide yourself from me." Jesse took hold of her hands, gazing the length of her as he did. "You're fucking beautiful."

"I'm fat."

Hands went around her and she cried out as he slapped her ass.

"Don't you ever call yourself that. You're fucking beautiful and I won't hear you saying anything else." The hand that slapped her gripped her flesh tighter. "So fucking full." He kissed her lips before sliding down to caress her neck.

His clothes were rough against her naked flesh. He moved behind her with his hands caressing up and down her body. "The clothes you wear are too big for such a curvy body." Staring straight ahead out of the window, she tensed as his hand cupped her naked pussy. "If men knew what an amazing body you had they would never leave you alone. You're going to drive me crazy."

Kisses rained down on her neck and shoulder.

"Now I'm going to see if you're wet for me."

Fingers separated the folds of her sex, sliding through. "That's right, baby, you're so wet for me. Do you want me? Do you want my cock inside your virgin cunt?"

The romance novels she'd been reading were of the erotic variety. His talk didn't offend her but excited her.

"I know what you're thinking. I did my research on those books, Piper. You're a hot woman at heart. You just need the right man to bring out your dirty side." He stroked her clit and she shuddered in his arms, unused to being touched by fingers other than her own.

"Jesse," she said, gasping for breath.

"If you're scared, tell me to stop. I'd never force you against your will."

"I don't want you to stop."

Once again he spun her to face him.

"Good, because I don't want to stop. You're mine now, baby."

She liked the idea of being owned by him.

"No other man knows your body. Only I want that pleasure, do you understand?"

"Yes."

"Good. Sit down on the sofa."

Stepping away from him, confused by his order, Piper took a seat on the sofa like he told her.

She stared up the length of him, watching as he tore his shirt off, revealing the many tattoos decorating his body. His arms were covered in different designs and his body was like a landscape of hell. The designs were perfect, not revolting.

"Why did you get these," she asked, reaching out to touch his chest. Heat radiated off him and the electricity from the touch made her gasp.

"I love getting ink. Haven't you ever thought about it, getting ink on your body?" he asked.

Piper shook her head. Letting anyone see her body was not high on her list of things to do by a certain age.

"We'll take care of that. I own you now. You're mine."

He'd spoken those words twice and each time gave her thrill.

# CHAPTER FOUR

Jesse's cock was so fucking uncomfortable in the tight jeans. He needed them off otherwise his shaft wouldn't be much use for anything, let alone fucking. Staring at Piper's naked body stirred an arousal deep inside him. Her touch sent fire swirling inside. Every woman he'd been with had given pleasure, which he'd taken. No woman had created a burning so bright he didn't think he'd last the first thrust.

She would be incredibly tight and hot. Fuck, she was a virgin. He needed to keep his wits about him otherwise her first time would end up being a nightmare.

"They're beautiful," she said. "Hard but beautiful."

"I've got a guy out in the sticks who keeps a clean shop. If you ever want one then I'll take you to him. He'd be the only one I trust with your body." Reaching out, he ran fingers through her hair then down her back, touching her.

All too soon, he withdrew and worked at the buckle holding the jeans up. Pushing the jeans down his thighs, he kicked off the boots and stepped out.

Her eyes were wide as she settled on his cock. Gripping the length, he brought his hand up and down, showing himself off to her.

"Do you like what you see?" he asked.

"You don't wear any underwear?"

"It irritates me." Kneeling before her, he caressed her smooth thighs, pressing her back against the sofa. "Stop thinking about everything. There's only us here, Piper. No one else."

Opening her thighs wide, he kept his gaze on her. He couldn't look away. She drew him in with her gaze alone. They had a connection that he couldn't break away from.

He touched her pussy, smelling her musky scent. Her eyes opened wide and Jesse decided to no longer play it safe."

Looking down her body, he stared at the jewel of her clit peeking out of its hood. She was soaking wet and by the time he was done with her, Jesse was determined to have her a quivering mess of need.

He leaned in close, holding the folds of her sex apart, exposing her slit.

Her stomach shook and her breathing grew deeper.

"You've got such a pretty pussy."

Jesse had been with his share of women to know a pretty pussy from an ugly one. She kept her bush nicely trimmed, which he liked. He hated women who shaved it all off. Ever since his first time with a woman, he'd loved fucking a woman, not a girl.

"You keep staring at it."

"Baby, I want to fucking eat you. It's taking all

my strength not to grab my cock and slam inside you." Glancing up, he smiled. "I'm going to take my sweet time with your pussy. I'll have you dripping wet and begging for my cock."

It was a promise he intended to keep.

Keeping his eyes on hers, he leaned down, never breaking contact as he swiped his tongue through her creamy slit. Piper closed her eyes. Focusing all of his attention on her sweet clit, Jesse licked up and down her slit.

He took his time, circling her nub before going down to tongue the entrance of her cunt. Gripping his shaft, he fisted the length while enjoying the feel and taste of her.

After several strokes, he released his cock then held onto her thighs.

Her fingers tightened on the edge of the sofa as her moans got louder.

"Jesse," she whimpered.

"I'm going to make you come, baby." Holding her hips, he slid her ass to the edge. Settling her feet onto his shoulders, he sucked on her clit as he stroked a finger against her virgin entrance, coating the digit with her cream.

The club, the plan and what he needed to get out of her was out of his mind. All he wanted to do was give her pleasure. Part of him wished he'd not entered her life with a plan of seduction. Piper deserved more and better.

Cutting the thought from his mind, he focused on giving her what she needed.

He cupped her ass, squeezing the flesh hard as he stroked her clit, tonguing her.

She was so close to the edge of bliss. He was determined to bring her over before he felt any pleasure of his own.

Piper cried out his name.

"Come for me, baby." He muttered the words against her nub, knowing she was so close.

"Please," she begged.

Focusing on her clit, he licked, sucked and nibbled on the tiny bud until she finally shattered underneath him. Her body jerked and Jesse held onto her hips, keeping her still as he brought her back down.

Wiping her juices from his chin, he leaned back, staring into her startled eyes. "What are you thinking, baby?"

"I've never felt anything like that," she said.

Picking her up, ignoring her squeal of protest, he carried her to his bedroom. All virgins deserved to be made love to on a bed, not on a sofa or inside a car.

"I'm too heavy." She held on. She clawed against his back. The burn from her nails turned him on even more.

Going to the drawer beside his bed, he pulled out a packet of condoms and some lube and dropped them to the bed. He always kept protection close by. Never had he fucked a woman without a rubber. The last thing he wanted was a woman claiming to be the mother of one of his brats, especially not the women begging to be his old lady at the club.

He climbed onto the bed, pressing between her thighs.

"Taste yourself," he said, pressing his lips to hers.

Piper was so relaxed. Her hands went around his neck, holding on as he deepened the kiss. The scent of her arousal surrounded him. She licked his lips, groaning as she did.

"You taste so fucking sweet." Biting down onto her bottom lip, he stared into her eyes, knowing he was ready to take her.

Pulling away, he tore into the silver foil packet, pulling out the condom and sheathing himself. Next, he squirted plenty of lube over his covered shaft.

"Why are you doing that?" she asked, staring up at him. She looked like a fucking goddess.

"You're going to be incredibly tight. I don't want to hurt you." He wasn't a small man and the last thing he needed to deal with was the look of pain on her face.

"Okay."

With her eyes on him, Jesse stroked his cock, smearing the lube over the length. Her gaze turned him on more. When he was satisfied with the added protection for her, he settled over her, keeping a firm grip on his cock. Pressing the head to her entrance, he stared into her eyes.

"If at any time you need me to stop, tell me."

He pushed the tip inside her. She tensed. Her hands went to his arms with nails biting into his flesh.

With the tip inside, he moved his hands to her hips and in one smooth thrust, he claimed her virginity and slammed in deep into her core. She cried out, gripping him tightly. He wasn't wrong.

Her cunt was so fucking tight and perfect. The ripples of her pussy, gripped him, drawing him in deeper.

Fuck, he'd never felt anything like it.

"It hurts. Please don't move." Tears clouded her eyes.

He felt like a fucking prick for not seeing the pain earlier. Holding still within her, he kissed her lips, caressing down to stroke her neck. In no time at all, she was whimpering underneath him, thrusting up to him, begging for him to fuck her.

Gripping her hip tightly, he pulled out of her tight heat only to slam back inside.

They came together hard and hot. Claiming her lips, Jesse plundered her mouth making love to her lips the same way he was fucking her pussy.

****

Piper was burning up from the inside out. His cock branded her like that of a hot poker. Her body was no longer her own but Jesse's to do as he would with. She cried out as he pulled out of her until only the tip remained then thrust harder than ever. Reaching behind her, she pressed her hands against the headboard, trying to stop her head from banging against it.

"Fucking tight and perfect. Best fucking pussy I've ever had."

She liked the way he was talking and she hated how weak she felt when it came to him. He set her body on fire as he fucked her hard. His lips were creating havoc with the rest of her body.

He turned them so they were facing each other on their sides. Fingers slid between them, going between her slit. "I want you to come before I do." Jesse kissed her neck, biting down onto her neck. She didn't think it was possible to come a second time.

Crying out, she was shocked as Jesse hurtled her over the edge into a second orgasm. Seconds later she heard and felt him find release. He tensed up, growling out her name, holding her tight almost bruising. His arms wrapped around her tightly.

Jesse kissed her lips, nudging her up to face him. "Thank you."

"What for?"

"Giving me your virginity."

"It doesn't mean anything," she said, feeling her cheeks heat.

"Means something to me, baby. Remember what I told you?"

Searching through her thoughts she recalled what he said. "You own me?"

"That's right, baby. You're mine."

He stroked her back, going down to squeeze her ass. Gasping, she stared into his blue depths feeling lost. "I don't know what to say."

"There's nothing to say." Locking their fingers together, he kissed her once again. Everything he did invaded her senses.

They stayed like that on the bed, locked together, kissing and smiling. Piper felt like she'd gone to heaven. For once in her life this man was paying attention to her instead of her father.

The sound of the telephone invaded their moment together.

"Shit, I forgot to phone my dad. He's probably worried sick."

"Easy, baby," Jesse said, pulling out of her body making her gasp. "I'll grab your phone."

He disappeared out of the bedroom and she grabbed the pillow to cover her nakedness. The ringing stopped as he walked into the room.

"I'll let you phone him and I'll run us a bath."

"Okay." She watched him leave her alone as the ringing started up again. "Hello," she said, answering on the third ring.

"Where are you?" her father asked.

"With a friend. I should have called." Glancing at the clock near his bed, Piper gasped. She'd been with Jesse three hours already. Running fingers through her hair, she tried to calm her nerves. Three hours of already being with him was insane.

"Should have called? My men have been worried sick. Never once have you disappeared from the fucking coffee shop without alerting us first. I've told you, Piper, to be fucking careful."

She heard the water running and her excitement spiked again.

"I'll not be home tonight or tomorrow. I'm staying with a friend." She blurted the words out, knowing there was nothing else she could do once they were out in the open.

"Who the hell is this man?"

"No one you know. Please, I've been the good girl for a long time. I've never let you down and I'm asking for these days."

Silence fell over the line. Jesse clearing his throat made her jump. Looking up at him, she smiled.

"Who are you with?" John asked.

"Someone I met. Please, Dad, trust me. I'm fine. I know what I'm doing. I'll see you soon." She hung up, turning the phone off so she wouldn't be tempted to answer the damn thing again.

"Are you being a naughty girl? Keeping me a secret from Daddy?"

His arms were folded over his chest. Staring down the length of his body, her cheeks heated at the sight of his hard cock.

"It's best he doesn't know anything." Gripping the pillow to her body tightly, she smiled at him. "We've not given each other any promises."

"No, it's good. I'm not ready to impress your father."

"Good." She loved her father but she knew he'd find some way of pushing Jesse away.

"Come on, baby. It's bath time."

He reached out for her. Taking his hand, she followed him into the bathroom. The large tub was filled with hot water, covered in a layer of bubbles.

"You'll be sore after your first time."

She got inside the tub and gasped as he climbed behind her.

Arms went around her body, pulling her close. The length of his cock settled against her ass.

"How are you feeling?" he asked.

"I'm fine. A little sore but overall I'm fine." Looking behind her, she caressed his cheek. "You worry a little too much. I'm a bit old to be a virgin. I'm glad it's over."

"Your old man, does he keep the men away?" Jesse reached over, taking hold of a sponge and some soap. She didn't move until he asked. Leaning forward, she pulled her hair down one shoulder.

"No, he doesn't keep them away at all." Thinking about the prom date, she felt sad all of a sudden. "In case you haven't noticed I'm not actually model material."

"You're beautiful, Piper. Your shape is perfect and I know I'm not the first man to think it."

He washed her body then coaxed her to lean back.

"My dad is the president of the Hell's Charter. It's a motorcycle group and for some reason men seem to think it's great to be part of it. The guys who try to date me are using my position in the club to get to my father." Piper went into more detail about how she'd been used by the men trying to get on her father's good side. She shook her head, recalling the numerous times they'd asked her to put a word in for them. "After some time I found it easier to not date."

"Those bastards didn't know what they were missing." His hands cupped her breasts, pinching her nipples. "They will never know how responsive your body is." He tweaked each bud then slid down to her thighs.

Gasping, she closed her eyes, waiting for him to continue speaking. His voice was hypnotic.

"No one but me will ever know how tight your cunt is or how you taste. I love licking your pussy, baby."

Fingers slid inside her as he caressed her clit at the same time.

Gripping the edge of the bathtub, she tried to keep some hold over her sanity. There was nothing left other than giving her body over to him.

With quick ease he washed her body then climbed out of the bath. He didn't wait for her to dry. Jesse picked her up, and settled her on the bed. She watched him grab another condom, tearing into the foil and then sliding it over his length.

"Get on your knees." The passion in his voice made her toes curl.

Going to her knees with her ass in the air, she gasped as his fingers teased through her slit, stroking her clit then sinking a finger into her cunt.

"So fucking tight." He kept repeating the words over and over.

In the next breath, he slid inside her. Crying out, Piper felt full from his possession. His cock jerked inside her. She felt every pulse as they cried out together.

"I'm never going to get tired of this. Your body is perfect for me, Piper."

Hands landed on her hips, drawing her in close. Jesse thrust inside her, hard, going deeper than she thought possible. He claimed her body easily. She no longer had control over herself.

Jesse was screwing her hard. Not only was he screwing her body but affecting her heart and mind. Over the last month, Piper had felt herself falling for him. He was the first man to ever continue pursuing her. After she turned him away, he kept coming back.

*No, I can't be in love with him.*

Even as she thought it, Piper knew it was true.

The man pounding inside her body was the only man she'd ever fallen in love with. Jesse had not only taken her virginity, he'd taken her heart along with him.

# CHAPTER FIVE

Jesse watched her cunt take him in. For the first time ever in his life, he wished he wasn't wearing a condom. He wanted to feel her naked cunt gripping him the same way she gripped his fingers. She'd be tight, wet and so welcoming.

Closing his eyes, he counted to three in an attempt to get his bearings with the onslaught of pleasure. Once he had himself under control, he reached over for the lube he'd used the first time he took her.

Pressing out the last drops of gel onto his fingers, he stroked his free hand over her ass. He hadn't been lying when talking about her body. She really was amazing. During his years at the Demons he'd fucked his fair share of women, slender, full, ugly and pretty. Piper was something else.

Even though she was born into the world of bikers she was still innocent to the core. She protected herself against the world by keeping them away. He'd broken through the wall, claiming her as his own.

*Is she really yours?*

The reason why he had her in the first place

invaded his mind. He felt like a fucking bastard for taking her virginity and he'd only been hunting for the information that Charley wanted.

*Get the information without her knowing. No one has to know why you're here.*

"Jesse, are you all right?" she asked. He'd paused mid-thrust.

Stroking a hand down her back and staring at where she took his cock to the puckered entrance of her ass, Jesse couldn't help but nod. "Yeah, I'm fine."

Inside he was in turmoil. Cutting everything off other than the pleasure, he slid back inside her pussy as he caressed her asshole.

She tensed but he soothed her gently. "It's okay, baby. Give yourself to me."

Slowly, he got her to relax giving him what he wanted. He didn't press into her anus but he continued to fuck her with slow, even strokes.

Her moans were driving him crazy.

"I'm going to fuck you with my finger. I'm going to own this ass just like I own your cunt."

"Yes, Jesse."

Jesse had researched the books she read. Piper loved erotic literature and he'd read one of the stories to find plenty of anal sex descriptions. Even though she'd been a virgin, he sensed the need and lust within her. He was determined to open her up like a precious flower. Smiling, he pressed his index finger against the entrance to her ass. She resisted him at first, denying him access to her body. He didn't let up until he worked his finger into her ass.

Her pussy tightened around him, rippling around his cock.

"Touch your clit, baby. Show me how much you want my cock."

He watched her hand disappear between her thighs and felt the moment she touched her clit. The first stroke made her spasm around his shaft. Growling, he held onto her hip as he teased her ass.

"Do you like the feel of me inside your ass?" he asked, wanting to hear her scream with desire.

"Yes."

"Good. I'm going to fuck you here soon."

"Yes."

She cried out, moaning as he slapped her ass. The sight of his handprint sent him over the edge. Slamming inside her, over and over again, he tensed as his come filled the condom.

Jesse heard her join him seconds later, pulsing around his cock as she did.

"That's it, baby. Give it to me. Come all over my cock." Pumping in and out of her ass he waited for her to finish with her release.

Easing a second finger inside her ass, he got her used to the feel of him. Only when she collapsed to the bed completely spent did he pull out of her. Going to the bathroom, he stared at his reflection, hating what he saw. Washing his hands, he tried to ignore the guilt at what he'd done to her.

Other men had used her to get to her father. He was no different, only he was using her to get information out of her. Taking the warm cloth he'd wrung out, he went back to her. Jesse cleaned her up quickly before throwing the cloth in the wash basket and holding her in his arms. Her head rested on his chest with her fingers following the lines of his ink.

"Do you think I should get a tattoo?" she asked.

"Only if you want to." He held her close. With other women he got them out of his room as soon as possible. Jesse wasn't ignorant to the fact he didn't want to push Piper away.

"What do you do for work?" she asked, looking up at him.

"I'm a mechanic. What about you?" He needed to steer the conversation toward her.

"I work for my dad. Club business and handling the books."

He paused, wanting to find out the information Charley had sent him on and not wanting to know at the same time.

*Get the information and work on getting her to fall for you.*

Jesse frowned. No, he didn't want Piper to fall in love with him. What he wanted was for when they parted Piper wouldn't be hurt by what he'd done if she ever found out the truth.

"Sounds interesting."

"Not really. I deal with figures and Dad asks me to make files up on some of our new boys. He doesn't like to take on any new member who's a snitch or from another club."

His heart was pounding. Stroking her side he tried to think of something more to say. He never believed getting a woman to speak was in bed.

"Do you off people like they say in the movies?" He chuckled, forcing himself to make the conversation light.

"Nah, Dad's not a murderer. Well, I've never seen him kill anyone and anyway, I don't get drawn into that at all. I'm always in the office or I cook for the boys."

"Is that the reason you got all the beef?" he asked.

"Yeah. The guys wouldn't appreciate vegetables or pasta. They demand meat and potatoes and in bulk." She chuckled.

"What about your mother?"

"I never knew her. Dad said he loved her but she didn't stick around." She paused and he wondered what she was thinking about. "He got angry recently. There was this new guy. Junior. He was sniffing around something. I had to get a background check on him or something."

The mention of Junior had Jesse tensing.

"Why would he do that?"

*Be cool.*

She leaned up staring down at him. "You can't say anything to anyone, okay?" He nodded. "I think Junior was playing the books. He was telling Dad one thing while in the next something else. None of his stories added up."

"Playing the books? Maybe you've been reading too many stories. You're creeping me out," Jesse said. He had all the information he needed from her.

Piper giggled. "Maybe you're right."

"Come on, I think it's time for us to get some food. Do you want to head to the kitchen and see what you can make? I'm going to change the sheets."

"Sure." She kissed his lips then walked out of the room.

Grabbing his cell phone he dialed Charley's number.

"What do you have?"

"Junior was screwing them over. She made a file up on him and John Rix believes he was lying. Is this what you need?" Jesse asked, wanting the charade to be over.

"I need more information but that's good. I'm going to give John a call and see what I can find out now."

"No war then?"

"I did ask Junior to find out what was inside John's books, his financials and deals, but I didn't ask him to take anything. I wanted to make sure John wasn't taking my deals from my fucking territory. I know John puts some people in our club to do the same. I don't mind but I've never killed one of his men."

"She doesn't know John killed Junior. Her area is figures and handling the business side of everything." He heard her humming in the background.

"Okay, I'm going to handle things now. You can get rid of her."

Charley hung up and Jesse placed the cell phone inside his drawer. Running a hand over his face, he realized he wasn't ready to get rid of her.

Heading out to the kitchen he found her stirring something in a frying pan. The smell of fried onions greeted him. She wore his shirt that he'd taken off before licking her out.

"Wow, something smells good already."

She looked up smiling. "I'm kept around to cook. It's something I love doing. Oh, and baking. I make a mean chocolate fudge cake."

"I can't wait to taste it." Wrapping his arms around her, he delved underneath the shirt to finger her tight nipples. "I tell you what else I can't wait to taste." Sliding a finger between her clit, he gathered her cream then sucked his finger clean of her juice.

"I'm never going to get used to you at all." She sounded breathless to him.

"Good. I'm going to keep you in a state of arousal. Your body is going to be craving me."

\*\*\*\*

Three hours later, filled with food and fucked into exhaustion, she followed the line of one of his tattoos that was interlocked with another. She'd never thought of having a tattoo before. He was leaning against the headboard, smoking a cigarette. Their legs were locked together and his hand rested on her ass. She liked how he kept touching her even when they weren't having sex.

"What's it like?" she asked, gazing up at him.

"What?"

"Getting a tattoo?"

He shrugged. "I don't know. I've not given it much thought. I like the burn of the needle. It's not for everyone." Jesse docked out his cigarette blowing the smoke up to the ceiling.

"I've really loved today," she said, tucking some hair behind her ear.

Jesse smiled. "Babe, the day's not even over. In fact, I've got a lot more fun planned before the end of the night."

Glancing at the clock she saw it was only a little after ten. He eased her over his lap to straddle him. His cock, which lay flaccid, rested against her pussy.

"Now, where were we?" Jesse cupped her breasts. He pinched her nipples and the arousal stirred within her. Flinging her head back she let out a moan. "God, I love your tits. You really need to get clothes that showcase these beauties." He paused, looking over her shoulder. "Actually, keep them covered. I don't want anyone to know how fucking sexy you are. You're mine."

Laughing, she cried out as his lips sucked on her nipples.

"Don't stop," she said, shuddering from arousal.

"I'm not going to." He moved to the next breast, then went back to the first one. She held onto his legs in the hope of keeping herself still. His tongue lapped at each nipple then sucked, biting down before he pulled away. "Take hold of my cock."

She grabbed his cock and followed his instructions, running her fingers down the length.

"Do you want me to fuck you or do you want to taste me?" he asked.

Licking her lips, Piper knew she wanted to taste him more than anything else. "I want to taste you."

"I love your answer, baby." He eased her off him and she was surprised by how easily he moved her.

Staring down at his hardening length, Piper felt nervous and foolish. She'd never sucked a man's cock before.

"Erm, I don't know what I'm doing. I've never done this before." Her cheeks had to be burning.

"I know, baby. Hold me, like this." Jesse wrapped his fingers around the base of his shaft, which held the length straight up.

She covered his fingers as he removed his hand. He felt strange, hard yet soft at the same time.

"Your fingers are a little cold," he said, smiling.

Jerking her hands away, she looked at him. "Crap, sorry, I didn't mean to hurt you."

"You didn't hurt me. Wrap your fingers around the base and feel me. Touch me, Piper." The need in his voice couldn't be disguised. Even she detected the need lurking within him.

Piper worked her fingers over his length, getting him hard. The tip leaked pre-come as the vein along the side pulsed with every beat.

"That feels so good, baby."

He was always calling her baby. She liked the name. Her father and the guys referred to her as honey or Piper. Baby...she liked it.

Leaning forward she liked the jewel of come off the tip. "Yeah, lick me clean, Piper. Tease me with your sweet lips."

Smiling, she took the head of him into her mouth. She flicked the tip then glided down, taking more of him. His hands fisted in the sheets on either side of him. The look in his eyes thrilled her. He appeared possessed by what she was doing with her lips.

"Fuck, yeah, baby, take more of me."

Eyes closed, Piper took more of his shaft into her mouth, sucking her cheeks in. Jesse growled. His hands sunk into her hair forcing her head down. She loved the feel of him taking control, forcing his way inside. He screwed her mouth but didn't make it uncomfortable for her.

Piper relaxed, letting him take over, claiming her mouth.

"So fucking beautiful. I can't believe this, pure heaven."

She smiled, loving everything he said and did.

"I'm going to come, baby. If you don't want my come then let up."

Piper kept sucking on him. Even though she'd been a virgin, Piper knew about sex. Her lack of sex life didn't mean she didn't know what happened during it. Working the root of his cock she felt the first blast of his semen hit the back of her throat. She had no choice other than to swallow him down.

Jesse screamed, cursed and gripped her hair tightly as he released into her mouth.

When there was nothing more, he tugged on her hair to pull her up. "Perfect," he said, slamming his lips down on hers.

She kissed him back, glowing from the inside out at his feelings. Piper was in love with him and it scared her. No woman should fall in love with a guy they'd slept with after knowing each other so little.

He pushed her to the bed and within seconds his tongue worked between her thighs. She cried out with each thrust and tease of his tongue. Jesse knew what he was doing. He sucked her clit as he pressed fingers inside her. The dual sensation was amazing and her climax took Piper by surprise. Thrusting up to his hand, she whimpered with need.

Kissing up her body he took her lips last. She tasted her essence on his lips.

"You're really something." He held her tightly against him.

"What do you mean?" she asked, basking in the glow of her orgasm.

"When tomorrow is over, I want you to take me to your father."

She tensed. What the hell?

"No, wait, this is not what you think." Jesse caught her arms, stopping her from pushing him away.

"You used me."

"No, I haven't used you." The moment he mentioned her father, she felt broken, torn in two. "I swear. I'm asking him permission to date you. I want him to know I'm not going away when it comes to you."

"Are you being serious?" she asked, wanting to trust him.

"Yes. This is real, Piper. You and me, I'm not giving you up."

She frowned. "Is this about sex or something?"

He laughed. "Baby, I wouldn't be controlled by sex. This is real. Haven't you liked my company this past month?"

"I've loved it. This makes no sense. We barely know each other."

Jesse shrugged. "Doesn't matter. We can get to know each other any time."

Biting into her lip she nodded her head.

"Now, I think it's time we get some sleep."

They lay together on the bed. His arms

surrounded her with warmth. Closing her eyes, she settled against him, not wanting their time to change. John would put Jesse through his paces and there was nothing she'd be able to do to stop it.

"Relax, baby. There's nothing to worry about," he said, whispering the words against her skin.

She relaxed in his arms, believing everything he said. For once she'd found a man who wanted her and not the club she'd been born into.

# CHAPTER SIX

Jesse woke up at seven in the morning knowing he needed to get in touch with Charley about what happened. Crap, he wished he hadn't fallen for the woman in his arms. One of her legs lay between his and her hand was spread out across his chest. In all of his life he'd never found any kind of relaxation with a woman in his arms. For the last twenty-four hours, Piper had broken down barriers he'd kept in place.

*I can't lose her.*

Closing his eyes, he tried to focus on his breathing so he wouldn't wake her. His cock had a mind of its own. Glancing down, his cock poked her in the side. Her breasts were pressed against his chest.

The more he thought about their time together the previous day the harder it was to gain control of his arousal.

*Down boy.*

"Morning," she said, moaning. He gazed at her, watching as she stroked his chest with her fingertips.

"Morning, baby."

"Do you need me to get off you?"

"Why?"

"You need to go to the toilet, right?"

He was confused for several seconds when her words suddenly dawned on him.

"What? No, baby, I'm turned on. I don't need to use the bathroom. Well, I do, but this is more about you."

"Oh." She jerked up, looking to his cock then to his face.

"I'm just going to the bathroom. Go ahead and put the kettle on. I'll finish when you use the bathroom."

"Okay." Piper kissed his lips then climbed off the bed. She didn't cover up her nakedness and he loved seeing her walk around his place.

*You're screwed.*

Ignoring the warning going off in his brain, he walked to the bathroom. Once he finished he took over, making coffee as Piper took his place. He slapped her ass on the way past, loving the sound of her squeal.

*Totally screwed.*

Jesse had fallen in love with her and he was totally, fucking screwed. John Rix would see through their chance meeting, which was one of the reasons why he wanted the opportunity to talk with him before Piper.

His cell phone was off in the bedroom. There was no way for him to get in touch with Charley without Piper finding out.

"Um, that coffee smells so good," Piper said, walking toward him. She'd put on one of his robes, covering her nakedness.

"Nah, I don't think so." He pushed the robe off her shoulders until it fell to the floor. Jesse stood naked and so did Piper now.

"Hey, I need that."

"No one is going to get the chance to see you naked, baby. We're alone and I'm off work. It's just the two of us." Wrapping an arm around her waist he tugged her close. Her tiny hand went to his chest. "And I can think of so many things I want to do to you." Slapping the cheek of her ass, he laughed at her squeak.

"Will you stop hitting me?" she asked.

"I'm spanking you, baby. I'm not hitting you."

"Either way, it stings."

Laughing, he took her lips, tasting the spearmint of the toothpaste she'd used. "You taste a lot better than any coffee." He put his cup down then lifted her up in his arms. She wasn't light but he didn't mind as he carried her back through to his bedroom.

"Hey, I want my coffee. I need my coffee."

"I'm going to be your coffee for the day."

He dropped her to the bed then grabbed another condom from the drawer.

The spare lube he kept glared up at him, begging to be used. Taking out the tube, he dropped it to the bed.

"I doubt you're going to keep me awake for the rest of the day."

Jesse pressed his palm to her pussy, feeling the slickness of her arousal.

She cried out. Chuckling, he slid a finger inside her cunt.

"I can keep you awake and I'll do a far better job than any caffeine hit."

Adding a second finger, he pushed into her body, watching her come apart beneath his hand. There was nothing false about her response to his touch. She was natural and perfect.

Gliding his thumb over her clit he watched her orgasm, feeling her cunt spasm around his fingers.

"That's it, baby. Give me everything. Your body knows who its master is."

Licking her cream off his fingers, he handed her the foil packet. "Put it on me."

She went to her knees before him, tearing into the foil packet then sliding the condom over his shaft. He waited for her to put the condom on him.

"Get on your knees and I want you to trust me. Can you do that?" he asked.

"Yes, I trust you."

"Good."

He caressed the cheeks of her ass, watching her shudder beneath his touch.

"I'm going to fuck your ass, baby. You can take me but I need you to trust me. I don't want to hurt you."

"I trust you, Jesse." He was sure she was going to say something else. Instead, she stayed quiet, leaving him to wonder what she would have said.

Picking up the tube of lubrication, he uncapped it and smeared plenty over his covered shaft. He wanted to make sure she was protected completely. He didn't want to hurt her.

Once his cock was covered with the lube, he squirted plenty against the puckered hole he wanted so much.

She gasped. "It's cold."

Running fingers through the gel, he started to press against her ass. She tensed, but slowly, Piper started to relax against him.

With the tip of his finger inside her ass, she tensed again. Soothing her with words, touches and patience, Jesse waited for her to relax once again before pushing deeper.

After some time she took all of his finger and then a second. When he worked a third finger into her ass, he knew she was ready to take his cock.

He gripped the root and pressed the head to her anus.

She tensed up again.

"It's only me, baby. Trust me. Let me claim you. Remember, I'm not letting you go."

Slowly, once again she relaxed against him.

Piper took the tip of his cock into her ass and he took his time to work in more of his length. She didn't scream or cry out at his penetration. Staying still under his claiming, Jesse worked his way inside her until she'd taken every single inch.

"I'm in, baby. You've got me all."

Opening the cheeks of her ass wide, he watched his cock inside her. It was one of the most erotic things he'd ever seen.

He'd claimed her. In his mind, Piper was his and no other man was ever going to know the kind of pleasure she could give. He would handle everything with John and his club.

"It feels weird," she said. She was breathless every time she talked.

"It'll get better." He was determined she'd love

it by the time he was finished. Pulling out of her heat, he started up a pace that took his time, getting her accustomed to the feel of him inside.

In no time at all, she was thrusting against him, begging and screaming for more. He fucked her hard, reaching around to strum her clit with every thrust he made.

Jesse knew he'd fallen deep and hard for this woman. He would put everything right and treat her like the princess she fucking deserved.

Slamming in deep, he fucked her hard, feeling the edge of bliss was close.

"Come for me, Piper. I need you to come before I find my own release." He yelled the words for her to hear over the erotic fog over them. Jesse couldn't hear anything past the beating of his heart and her screams of pleasure.

"I'm coming," she said, crying out.

He kept strumming her clit, feeling her orgasm wrapped around his dick. With two quick thrusts, Jesse followed her into bliss. The pleasure was unlike anything he'd ever thought.

Neither of them had time to bask in the arousal as his front door was slammed opened. Covering Piper's nakedness, he quickly tore the condom off, ready to take on any fucker who charged through his door. Whoever thought they could invade his home was fucking mistaken.

"Jesse, what's going on?" Piper asked, terrified.

She got her answer before he said anything.

John Rix charged through the bedroom door. The anger on his face was clear. John knew what had been going on as he looked between the two of them. Behind him Charley and a mixture of their boys crashed through the room.

He didn't defend himself as John landed a blow to his face. Not caring about his naked state, Jesse took the hit.

"You fucking piece of scum. You make me fucking sick." John landed a blow then another blow.

"Daddy, stop it." Piper had wrapped the blanket around her and was trying to tear her father off him.

Bless her, she didn't have a clue how much he deserved this beating.

"Get fucking dressed and get downstairs."

Jesse was pulled to his feet and dragged out of the apartment. A pair of jeans was handed to him.

The fresh air was freezing cold and he gasped, wishing he was back in his apartment wrapped around Piper.

****

She needed to get downstairs before her father hurt the man she loved. Drake, one of her father's boys, stood outside the bedroom giving her privacy to dress. She quickly pulled on a pair of Jesse's sweat pants and a shirt. Her sneakers were in the living room. Brushing past Drake, she quickly put the shoes on then headed downstairs.

"What were you thinking?" Drake asked, following her.

"I don't know what the hell is going on. I need to stop my dad before he does something stupid."

"You really don't know who that fucker is, do you?"

She stopped to look at him. "I don't have a clue what's going on but if you'd like to enlighten me, go ahead. I'm sure I could use the new info." Her hands were shaking and she was mortified inside at what her father had discovered when he'd walked into the bedroom.

Great, she didn't want her father knowing she'd experimented with anal sex. There was no hiding from it now.

Piper pushed the embarrassment aside and headed outside in time to see Charley, the leader of the Demon's, standing in front of Jesse who was on the floor, bleeding.

"You've made your point," Charley said.

"My daughter is not up for being played like some fucking tool. She doesn't know all of your men. You shouldn't have brought her into this." John's hands were fisted at his side.

She knew he was struggling to contain his anger, which was directed at Jesse.

"We needed information."

"Next time, you come to me. Don't send some fucking punk to screw with my daughter."

Her father's words cut her to the core. Jesse was staring at her, pleading almost. What the hell had happened? This morning she'd woken up so fucking happy and now she felt like she was being torn apart.

"What the hell are you trying to say?" Piper asked, turning her attention back to her father.

"This fucking asshole was using you, honey.

Yeah, he was sent on a mission to find out why we killed Junior. The little fucking weasel stealing our dough." John shouted the words for everyone to hear. Only the two MCs were present but that was still too many people for her liking. They'd seen her naked with Jesse.

Whirling around, she stared at Jesse. The shame on his face was clear to see. He didn't look away from her, either.

"Is this true?" She hated the hurt building inside her. Why was she really surprised? No one wanted her. She was the fat daughter of John Rix. She was a means to an end. In that moment, Piper hated herself and the life she'd started to lead.

"It started out that way. They needed information and you were the one we thought would have it."

Tears spilled from her eyes. She felt them falling, thick and fast. Again, she'd been used again to get to her father's club.

"You screwed me to what? To butter me up so I'd tell you all of my father's secrets?" she asked. "I don't know everything about the club."

"It started out like that but it changed, Piper. Surely you felt it."

"What? When you screwed me and all the time you were only wanting information?" Staring up and down his body, she didn't know if she even knew him. Everything he said was a lie.

"It's different, Piper. I love you. I'm telling you to trust me."

She shook her head. "No, I can't trust you. You're a fucking liar." Walking toward him, she stood in front of him then slapped him around the face. "Don't you ever come near me again. I don't want you near me. Do you understand?"

"Piper, please."

Spinning on her heel, she went to her father. "Get me out of here, please."

"Sure thing." John draped his arm over her shoulder. "We'll talk soon." His comment directed at Charley.

She didn't look back at the man who'd torn out her heart. Going toward her father's bike, she climbed on the back after putting on the helmet. Holding onto her father, she'd never been more happy to leave a man behind.

Jesse had hurt and humiliated her. She wouldn't be forgetting about this moment for a long time. When they got to the Hell's Charter clubhouse, she handed her helmet back and walked in. Several of the guys were playing pool. They looked at her as she entered. Without looking them in the eye she passed the sweet butts and old ladies, going to the back of the house to where her bedroom was.

Closing and locking the door, she went straight to the en-suite bathroom, scrubbing off any memory of Jesse's touch.

With the water cascading down around her, she gave into her tears. Pressing a hand to her face, she tried to stop the tears but couldn't.

She'd given her virginity to a man who'd only been using her to get what he wanted.

*Get over it. No one else cares.*

When she could cry no more, she turned the

water off, dried her body and put a nightshirt on. Brushing her hair, she settled on her bed, wishing the pain would go away.

Several people knocked, asking if she was all right. She heard the sweet butts giggling. The tears fell down her cheeks.

Her father didn't knock. He used the spare key to get inside.

"Honey, you shouldn't be alone." John locked the door behind him, moving toward the bed.

The tears continued to fall even though she wiped them away.

"I don't want you in here."

"I'm not going anywhere. This boy is different from all of the others." He sat down on the edge of the bed.

"I fell in love with him," she admitted.

"Shit, baby. I'm so sorry."

"Don't be. I should have known. A guy like that would never go for a girl like me."

"What the hell are you talking about? You're a beautiful woman, Piper. I know most of my boys would have you in a heartbeat if you ever showed them any interest."

"I'm fat, Dad. Men like thin women. Slender and model-like. I'm none of those things."

John cursed. "Honey, your mother wasn't slender. Yeah, some guys like fucking a stick but there are plenty of men who love a full woman with curves." He held her close. She remembered all the times over the years he'd comforted her after being bullied at school. "Any man would be happy to have you and you point the evil bastards out to me who wouldn't."

She chuckled. "I thought he was different."

"Maybe he was. I don't know, honey. I guess we'll see what happens and what he does."

"What do you mean?" she asked.

"If he really wants you, there will be no stopping him from coming to claim you."

Snuggled up against her father, Piper felt a little better. Over the years he'd always taken care of her, even when there was nothing he could do.

"I don't think he will."

"He looked upset, Piper. I think he'll surprise you."

"No, I'm not going to risk it." Pulling away from him, she wiped under her nose. She was done with being sad about the situation. Piper tucked her hair behind her ear and smiled at her father. "I'm sorry for putting the club at risk."

"Fuck the club. You're my little girl. No one hurts you. The guys would agree with me."

"I'm not going to break. I'm fine." The lies were pouring out of her mouth. She was breaking apart inside and it hurt every second she took a breath. John left her alone and she was free to finally break apart. No one else tried to bother her.

# CHAPTER SEVEN

"You can't keep me away from her, John. She's my fucking woman." Jesse yelled the words across the parking lot. He'd driven to the Hell's Charter clubhouse only to be held back by the entire club. They all looked at him as if he were scum. For the last week he'd been trying to get in touch with Piper with no luck. It was like she'd disappeared off the face of the earth. His boys stood behind him, giving him support and protection if any of the rival club members tried anything.

He didn't care what they tried. Jesse wanted his woman back. Her routine had changed in the last week. She no longer went to the coffee shop on Monday or Friday. Her phone was dead all the time.

"Who the fuck do you think you are?" John asked, stepping in front of all of his men.

"She's my woman." He slammed a hand against his chest.

"She's my fucking daughter and you've hurt her more than any other man I know. How dare you come to my land and start trying to yell at me."

John advanced, holding a baseball bat.

"Go on, John, kill the lad."

The distance between them thinned. Jesse wasn't afraid. Piper was worth fighting for. He wore his Demons cut along with his golden jewelry he liked. In his back pocket was the gold band he'd bought in the city. He intended to make Piper his wife.

"What the hell are you doing here, lad? My girl has been crying her eyes out over you. I told you to give her time," John said, lowering his voice so it was only between them.

"I'm going to marry Piper. I'm not here to cause a problem. I want her as my wife." He didn't raise his voice. This conversation wasn't going any further.

"Is this some game Charley's playing?"

"No, I don't care about merging the clubs. I only care about Piper."

"What do you want, Jesse?" Piper's voice invaded the tension. She stood on the edge of the group with her arms folded. The clothes she wore didn't do her body justice. The sight of her sent a shockwave to his gut. She looked so sad with her arms crossed over her stomach.

"I need to talk to you," he said, turning his attention back to her.

"What about?"

"We need to go somewhere private."

"No. Anything you need to say to me can be done in front of the men. I'm sure everyone is very busy and wants to move on with their day." She was cold. He saw it in the way she held her body. The tightening of her arms, and the shudder running through her showed the chill getting to her. She needed a coat.

"You want me to say everything in front of all of these men?" Jesse asked.

"Yes. They know you more than I do." She pointed toward his leather cut. "I didn't even know you were a member of the Demons. See, a lot I don't know about you, including your last name."

"Name's Jesse Jenkins. I've been a member of the Demons for the last ten years and I'm totally in love with you." The words blurted out before he could stop them. The desperation clawed at him. Losing Piper was not an option.

"What?"

"I love you. Yes, I'm not going to deny the fact I started pursuing you because I wanted to know about Junior but I fell for you."

"You screwed me for information," she said, spitting the words at him.

Was he a freak to find her anger a turn on?

"No. I screwed you because I wanted to." Guns were loaded and aimed at his head. "I got the information because none of our clubs want a war."

"I can't believe you." She turned on her heel, heading in the opposite direction. He looked at John, who gave him the nod to follow her.

"Believe what you want." She was heading toward the side of the clubhouse where she'd appeared from. "Piper, fucking stop."

She stopped suddenly, turned and glared at him. "I work for my father. I'm not part of club business. You should have stayed well away."

Going to his knees, he lifted the box containing

the gold ring he'd purchased for her. Piper shut up. Her gaze landed on the velvet box to his eyes and back again.

"What are you doing?" she asked.

He heard the sound of the boys joining them. Jesse didn't care what they thought of him for begging his woman. One week without her was too fucking long. "I want you to marry me. This is what I have to do. I get down on one knee but seeing as I pissed you off I'm actually on two knees." He tapped each knee for her to see. "I fucked up. I admit that but if I have to I'd do it all again because it brought me you. I love you, Piper."

Her eyes glazed over, tears forming.

"I can't believe you."

"Then give me time." He stood, taking the steps to close the distance between them. "I'm promising you a lifetime commitment. There's no other woman for me. I know my mind. Give me time."

Jesse wished for her to say yes. This had to be the hardest proposal in the history of all proposals. It sucked, but he knew it was the way it had to go. He'd fucked up, screwed her over, and this was the price he needed to pay.

"I don't know what you want from me," she said. "None of this is making sense. I can't trust you. This means nothing to me."

"I know you feel something for me." Reaching out, he stroked her cheek. He blanked out the whole world. None of their clubs existed, only the two of them in this moment. "I'm asking you to marry me. I want to make you my woman, my old lady. Please, give me a chance to prove I can do this."

Taking her hand he slid the ring onto her finger. It was a perfect fit.

"One chance, Piper. All I'm asking is for one chance. What we felt together, that was real." He gritted his teeth, hating how silent he needed to be about their time together. Jesse didn't want the other guys to know how responsive she was or how she sucked cock like an angel. All of these traits were his own.

"Fine, you want a chance then I'll give you a chance." She pulled away from him and before he could stop her, Piper kneed him in the balls.

Dropping to his knees, Jesse watched her walk toward the door.

"If you're really serious about this then you'll come and pick me up for coffee this Friday."

****

*Four months later*

Piper stared down at the books in front of her. Tapping the pencil on her lip she looked at the numbers as she worked out the sum.

"Are you going to give that boy a break?" John asked, walking into the office, taking a seat opposite her.

"What do you mean?" She'd been dating Jesse for the past four months. No sex, only dating and the odd kiss. Her body ached for something more but she was determined to not give in.

"I feel sorry for the boy. You're being a right bitch to him. When are you going to give the guy a break? Four months is a long time, honey."

Placing the pencil on the desk, she smiled at him. "I sometimes forget what went on between us. He comes around so often it's like he's part of the family."

"Jesse's not one of my boys. He's staying with the Demon's. You'll be a Hell's Charter princess, honey. Both clubs will look out for you. We're all excited about this."

"Dad, I was going to accept his marriage proposal tonight. He's making me dinner at his place. I'm going to accept and everything is going to be fine. Stop worrying." She reached over to tap his hand, fondly. "I love you too, Dad."

"I want what is best for you. I hate Jesse for what he did to you but I can see he's telling the truth. Boy loves you."

Piper smiled. "I'm starting to get it. Jesse is a hard ass who finally fell in love."

Over the last few months she heard a lot of women talking about Jesse Jenkins, stud muffin, being tamed by a biker princess. Every time she heard it, the news made her smile. She'd tamed a man. It was the strangest thought in the world.

"Well, good. I'll let the boys know what's going on."

He got up to leave.

"You do that."

Going back to her numbers, she wasn't expecting the knock on the office door. Looking up she saw Jesse, his arms folded, waiting for her.

"Hey, baby," he said.

Ever since he' d gone back to wearing his leather cut and displaying all of his muscle she'd struggled to string together a coherent thought.

"Hey yourself."

For Christmas both clubs had mingled at the Hell's Charter clubhouse. She'd cooked three turkeys and put a feast on that would make any chef proud. He'd worn the silver cross she'd given to him around his neck. Jesse owned so much gold jewelry she wanted hers to stand out against all the others he owned.

Jesse had bought her an e-reader, which she loved so much.

"Are you ready to go home?" he asked.

Glancing around her office she nodded, feeling nervous at being alone with him. For the last four months he'd really shown her how much he loved her. He told her every chance he got and he seemed to enjoy taking her around to his clubhouse.

"Yeah, I'm ready."

Grabbing her bag she followed him out. Several of the guys shook hands with Jesse on the way out. Her father raised an eyebrow at her. Glaring at him, she kept up with Jesse. His bike waited for them outside. Jesse strapped her bag to the back of the bike then handed her a helmet. She held onto him very tightly as he drove out of the club.

He smelled amazing.

When he was parked she climbed off and handed him his helmet. Jesse took her hand, leading her up to his apartment. Neither of them spoke and the tension built. She was surprised by the scent of chicken permeating the place.

"You cooked?"

"Yeah, I've been single for a long time and I know how to cook. I can follow a recipe." She chuckled, taking a seat as he opened the oven.

Piper watched him buzz around the kitchen getting their meal ready. She was totally in love with him and her father's words came back to haunt her. Was she being cruel in waiting to tell Jesse?

They all made mistakes and Jesse had paid long enough.

"Yes," she said, finally answering his questions.

"What, babe?" He put the casserole on the counter, staring at her.

"Yes, I'll marry you."

"Are you shitting me?"

"I hate that word but, no, I'm not shitting you, Jesse. I'm being serious. I want to marry you." He rushed around the counter, picking her up and pressing her against his chest.

"Fuck, I love you so fucking much." His lips slammed onto hers and he plunged his tongue into her mouth.

She whimpered, wrapping her arms around him.

"What about dinner?" she asked. He kissed down her neck sucking on her flesh.

"Fuck dinner." He left her side to put the casserole back in the oven.

In the next breath he was tearing at her clothes.

"Jesse, what are you doing?" She was laughing as he did.

"I've waited too fucking long to be inside you. I can't wait another fucking minute." Within seconds he slammed inside her. He had her perched on the edge of the stool. She was surprised by the power of his thrusts.

Crying out, she held onto him as he fucked her hard.

"Fuck, I forgot the condom."

"I don't care, don't stop." She'd been on the pill since she was young to help regulate her periods.

"Yeah." He gripped her hips slamming inside her, over and over again. "Fuck, I'm not going to last. Touch yourself. Make yourself come all over my fucking cock," he said.

She stroked her clit, feeling her orgasm approaching within seconds.

They both reached their climax together, shaking in each other's arms.

"I'm so sorry I fucked up, baby. I promise you, I won't do that again."

Pressing a finger to his lips, she silenced him. "Shut the fuck up, Jesse." Kissing him back, she moaned as his cock twitched inside her. "I don't want to hear anything else other than you fucking me and loving me."

"Baby, I'm going to spend the rest of my life fucking you, screwing every inch of this body."

He picked her up. Wrapping her legs around his waist, Piper moaned as he proved to her over and over that his stamina was something to be in awe about.

# EPILOGUE

*Ten years later*

"Come here, you little shit," Jesse said, shouting toward his five-year-old son, who was running around the yard. Piper loved this house and he couldn't deny her anything. Charley and John had helped with the down payment for the mortgage and together they'd paid him back. After ten years together they had four children to their name with a fifth on the way. David, Lily, Markus and Peter were the second best part of his life. Piper was the best thing that ever happened to him.

"Stop swearing at your son." Piper walked out of the kitchen with their three-year-old on her hip. Her stomach was barely rounded, as she was only a few months along. When she turned to grab a toy from the floor he saw the ink she'd gotten three months after they married. She'd kept asking him questions about his tattoos and he'd booked her an appointment. His name was there for him to see, showing who owned her. Piper never wore his leather cut but she had his name on her skin, turning him the fuck on.

"He's stolen my keys. I can't deal with the fucking stress if he tries to ride away." Running fingers through his hair, he looked at the plastic house he'd bought for the garden. Assembling the climbing frame had taken him and three of the guys to put right.

"Markus, get over here now. Don't make me tell you twice or your toys are confiscated," Piper said.

His woman was so totally sweet and yet their kids ever questioned her. She was the force to be reckoned with. Markus climbed out of the house and handed the keys over to his mother. "Why did you take them?" she asked.

"Daddy's going out. He shouldn't be going out."

"Honey, the boys are on their way over her. Daddy needs to go to the store to grab more burgers. You know how Grandpa John and Uncle Charley love their meat."

Markus crossed his arms and looked every so sad.

"Tell you what, little man, I'll take the truck and we'll go together."

"Yippee."

His son ran away, leaving him alone with his woman and Peter.

"You spoil them too much."

"I'm going to get us something for tonight. I'm thinking some chocolate ice cream and whipped cream," Jesse said, pressing his hand to her stomach.

"Why would you be doing that?" Piper asked. He saw the interest in her eyes. They rarely got time alone with all their kids. Thankfully, he'd spoken with John who agreed to take their four kids.

"Tonight, you, me, a bed and my stiff cock will be having some fun."

Piper covered Peter's ears. "You shouldn't be saying stuff like that."

He leaned in close so only she could hear. "Then start thinking about being fucked, baby. I'm going to screw you in every single room of this house. You won't be able to go anywhere without thinking about me and my cock." Kissing her cheek, he pulled away. "I'll see you when I get back."

Jesse's cock thickened to an unbearable point and he knew he was screwed himself. Piper had exploded into his life and he was so fucking happy.

**Sam Crescent** is passionate about fiction. She loves a good erotic romance and so it only made sense for her to spread her wings and start writing. She began writing in 2009 and finally got that first acceptance in 2011. She loves creating new characters and delving into the worlds that she creates. When she's not panicking about a story or arguing with a character, she can be found in her kitchen creating all kinds of havoc. Like her stories the creations in the kitchen can be dubious but sometimes things turn out great.

For more information on other books by Sam, visit her official website: SamCrescent.Wordpress.com

## Also by Sam Crescent

### *Evernight Publishing*

*Trapped Between Two Alphas*
*Hope*
*Expecting The Playboy's Baby*
*Just Friends*
*Time To Play*
*Learning To Forgive*
*His To Control*
*The Bad Boy's Reluctant Woman*
*Seducing Her Beast*
*Lash*
*Murphy*
*Nash*
*Tiny*
*Devil's Charm*
*The Alpha's Toy*
*Alpha Bait*
*Falling for the Enemy*

### *Secret Cravings Publishing*

*The Taking of Clara*
*Bend to His Will.*
*A Wild Older Woman*

CPSIA information can be obtained at www.ICGtesting.com
Printed in the USA
LVOW10s0241150616

492674LV00001B/5/P